Vampiro and Other Strange Tales of the Macabre

Vampiro and Other Strange Tales of the Macabre © 2019 Kevin J. Kennedy

Cover design by Michael Bray

All rights reserved. No part of this publication may be reproduced, distributed, or transmitted in any form or by any means, including photocopying, recording, or other electronic or mechanical methods, without the prior written permission of the publisher, except in the case of brief quotations embodied in critical reviews and certain other non-commercial uses permitted by copyright law.

First Printing, 2019

Other Books by KJK Publishing

Anthologies

Collected Christmas Horror Shorts

Collected Easter Horror Shorts

Collected Halloween Horror Shorts

Collected Christmas Horror Shorts 2

The Horror Collection: Gold Edition

The Horror Collection: Black Edition

The Horror Collection: Purple Edition

The Horror Collection: White Edition

100 Word Horrors

100 Word Horrors: Part 2

100 Word Horrors: Book 3

Carnival of Horror

Novels, Novellas & Collections

Pandemonium by J.C. Michael

You Only Get One Shot by Kevin J. Kennedy & J.C. Michael

Screechers by Kevin J. Kennedy & Christina Bergling

Dark Thoughts by Kevin J. Kennedy

Acknowledgements

I'd like to thank the following people for being part of my journey on this crazy writing trip. Brandy Yassa, Weston Kincade, J.C. Michael, Christina Bergling, Michael Bray, Lisa Vasquez, Becky Narron & Lisa Lee Tone. I'd like to thank the following authors for being part of the reason I write. Richard Laymon, Edward Lee, Ray Garton, Jack Ketchum, Carlton Mellick III, Iain Rob Wright, Jeff Strand & George Lennox, and last but not least. I'd like to thank the people who make everything worthwhile. My wife, my mum, my dad and my step daughter. I'm sure there will be lots of people I have forgot to mention. It's the main reason I rarely do these things. A special thanks to Brandy Yassa for doing the initial edits on this book and for Ann Keeran and Darren Tarditi Wilson for stepping in to finish them up when Brandy was otherwise engaged.

Table of Contents

The Games - Page 9

Thirteen Voices - Page 33

Don't Grass - Page 43

Would You Sell Your Soul? - Page 83

Vampiro - Page 95

A Town Called Easter - Page 117

Christmas in Hell - Page 149

The Games

By

Kevin J. Kennedy

The anticipation in town was at an all-time high. Every year on the 3rd of March the Braided Pony would put on various events for those in town who enjoyed partaking in the wilder side of things. The town was not what you would consider respectable by any means, but a lot of the town folk would avoid the events and let the more unruly have their fun. It was only one day a year after all.

The events had been going on for years now, and while they may have put many off from going near the establishment, it also meant that many others would come from miles away just to partake in the craziness and often stay on for quite some time, some never leaving. Last year's events had been the wildest yet but there was promise that this year would be even crazier.

It was only sunrise and the main street was already buzzing. Most of the men in the street were already drinking whatever they had left over from the night before to take the edge off. Only one of the working girls from the Braided Pony had made it out onto the street so far. Anyone who knew Sally-Ann knew that she would be part of the events but she knew that there was always time to turn a quick buck before she was too busy and before the other girls got there. Besides she was paid well for taking part in the games and her clientele always seemed to have a boost in the weeks afterwards. The staff were all outside setting up. There were tables lined along the front of the wooden structure that would serve as a makeshift bar. The bar staff were making their way in and out carrying various bottles of spirits that would need replenished several times during the day ahead. Some of the staff were setting up the equipment required for the events and challenges that would take place well into the night. The men who were already there were watching to see if they could work out what each stall would be and try and guess as to what would take place at them. Not everyone who attended was brave or stupid enough to participate. Most would just watch and drink but some of the men knew that at one point throughout the day they would be trying to win at least one of the prizes.

In previous years the events had prizes such as free drink for anything from an hour to a week, depending on how challenging the task was that they completed or won. Some of the events were aimed to shock or disgust while others were literally a matter of life and death. The participants usually fell into two categories, the young and dumb or the old with nothing to lose. Of course there were others. There was the odd lunatic who would do crazy shit on a day- to- day basis with no prize in sight and random others who just thought they had it in the bag. This year had promised to be the most spectacular yet but that was what they advertised every year. The owners of the Braided Pony rarely failed to meet expectations, however. It was all anyone who had been there talked about for weeks afterwards.

The horses normally tied up at the front of the bar had all been moved around back and the water troughs taken with them. Makeshift posters had been put up at some point through the night all along the main street. The sun beat down causing perspiration to drip from all who weren't hidden in the shade.

As the next two hours passed by the crowd built and had already began to work the bar staff. The stalls were all set and everyone was waiting for old Stan to arrive and start proceedings. Old Stan was said to be the owner of the Braided Pony but no one ever saw him apart from one day every year when the games took place. Some assumed since he was the owner he had no need to work in the establishment, while others found it extremely strange that he was only seen one day a year.

By noon the crowd was already well oiled and starting to get impatient. Everyone wanted to watch the first contest but with Stan nowhere in sight, they knew it would be a waiting game. The bar-staff were always wary because the one day you could count that the sheriff would not be seen was today. Just as arguments were beginning to break out, Stan appeared from nowhere, as always. He quickly hopped up on one of the bar tables and addressed the crowd.

"Ladies and gentlemen, thank you kindly for your patience." He paused for a second looking around the crowd as the noise died down and all eyes turned to him.

"I'm sure you all know this is going to be a very special day. Like always, I am sure you will find today's events more spectacular than last year. I only hope that some of you have the balls to take part."

As Stan paused this time the crowd went into an uproar, throwing their hats in the air, tossing drinks, a few people fired towards the sky. Stan used almost the same speech every year but it got them going. No one who came liked to be thought of as gutless but most would never consider participating.

As the cheers died down Stan continued, "We have some new games and contests for you all and we have some fantastic prizes. For those of you just watching you are in for a treat. For those of you taking part, not so much. But if you win... Well, you all know how we treat our winners. So, without further ado, do we have two contestants for our first competition?" The crowd went wild again. The first competition was always a wild card. No one was told which event would be first and often the men who had been there from sunrise were unable to even guess as to what each event entailed. It was normally two young bucks trying to make a name for themselves or impress a young lady.

There were somewhere between one hundred to two hundred people in the street, some of which were women or working girls. Neither took part. The women were there to work or spectate. This was a day for the men who wanted to prove something. Several of the younger lads called out and jumped up and down trying to be seen. Stan surveyed the crowd before pointing at two of the lads, "You and you," he said, as smiles appeared on both lads faces as they pushed their way to the front. The crowd went wild. Stetsons were thrown in the air as were drinks and as always, another few gun shots rang out.

The first table was all set up but had been covered by a blanket. The two young lads arrived in front of it and smiled sheepishly at Barbarella Lichtenstein. Barbarella was the oldest working girl in the Braided Pony by quite a bit but her gargantuan breasts, that always spilled over the top of her breathtakingly tight corset, had taken many a man's weekly wage in an hour or two. She smiled back at the boys knowingly and asked, "So, which of you two, big strong strapping lads is going to win a night with Babs?" Neither lad answered as they were both tongue- tied as well as thinking about the task ahead. Not that anyone really cared what Babs said. Their eyes were going between the wonderful cleavage and the covered table. Babs, knowing their minds were on the prize ahead and knowing the crowd was waiting in anticipation, pulled the table back to reveal two bowls of large raw bison bollocks. The face of both lads dropped. It was rare that the first challenge was an eating one. Often it would start off with something simple like a fist fight or quick draw competition but Stan had decided to switch it up this year. Neither lad had wanted to eat any of the disgusting treats that were often a part of the events but now they were in front of the table they had little option. Losing at one of the competitions often came with weeks of ribbing but that could be brushed off by mentioning that the person attempting to bring you down did not participate at all. Walking away from an event, without ever taking part in it, after you volunteered would mean you would be leaving town before sundown or stay and be a figure of ridicule for the rest of your life.

"Now boys. I'm not shy when it comes to working my way round a set of balls but we decided to give you two sets each. Tuck in." Babs said with a smile.

The two lads looked at each other before turning back to the table. The crowd fell almost silent apart from a few mumbles as they watched eagerly. A few shouts were called out. "Remember and cup the balls son" and "a gentle tickle works a treat" which set the crowd off. An awful smell wafted off the balls from sitting in the sun for a while, even though they were covered. The first lad called Sam decided his best chance was to just go for it so he scooped up the first lukewarm testicle and bit into it. It filled his hand and the spermatic cord hung between his fingers. It took everything he had to swallow it back. The other lad named Billy decided if he was going to participate he wanted to win so he scooped up his first ball and bit into the tough tissue and muscle while keeping his eyes firmly on Babs cleavage.

As the contest progressed both lads were sick, which was totally fine. As long as whatever went into their mouth was swallowed and went down for a few seconds before it came back up, they were still in. By the time Sam had made it to his forth testicle he was leaning over the table, sweat dripping from his brow and his stomach was doing summersaults. Billy was on his knees with massive stomach cramps from all the heaving but still managed a large last bite of his third testicle. Babs looked over at Stan who still stood on the bar table watching and he gave her a nod. Babs slipped her fingers into the top of her corset and slipped it down a bit allowing her massive breasts to spill over and hang down unflatteringly, like two rain drops, ready to snap and fall from a gutter. It was not an appealing site but both lads had heard stories about how she could literally wrap them right around your cock and perform a titty fuck like no one else. With renewed vigour Sam tucked back in to the meaty, sinewy muscle that was held in his hand. With a goal in sight he was able to push his mind away from what he was doing long enough to finish the bowl. He tried to stand straight and put his hands in the air as the winner. He lasted an entire second before his stomach turned over and he sprayed his entire feast over Babs drooping tits.

Now things like this happened often to the whores in the Braided Pony and some of the younger girls took whatever shit the guys gave them but not Babs. Winner or not she picked up the glass of Gin and Tonic she had sitting on the table and smashed it in his face. The glass shattered, cutting her hand to ribbons and turning Sam's face into a bloody shredded mess. As he hit the ground, screaming and Billy turned towards him, Babs grabbed Billy's hand and thrust it in the air. In most places, the unfairness of what happened would cause an uproar but not in this town. The crowd loved it and went wild.

Stan, still on his table, above the crowd started to speak. "Well, it looks like we have our first winner." As Stan spoke Babs was already leading Billy towards the Braided Pony. He followed with a stupid look on his face while still holding his stomach. "Are you all ready for the next competition?" Again, the crowd went wild.

The next few hours passed in a similar fashion, with a mixture of naive young lads or stupid old men entering competitions for prizes that really weren't worth all that much and completely humiliating and degrading themselves. As it approached sundown the tables lining the outside of the Braided Pony were covered in both blood and sick. Arguments had broken out and the men had fought with both knives and guns, which was always the case on this day every year. The competitions had been varied and increasingly sickening as the hours had passed from noon. The men had eaten out whores with blue waffle disease, knelt while old broken down whores had stuck fingers down their own throats and vomited into the men's mouths. Five loads the winner took and they weren't allowed to bring anything back up in that one. There was a competition where the men had to bury their arm in a cows arse up to the shoulder, swap over and do it with the other arm and then have a fist fight. It didn't do much other than give them stinky fists but the smell was pretty powerful and while taking a punch was normally bad enough these men had to take punches and ended up wrestling on the ground covered in cow shit. The crowd seemed to enjoy that one.

The penultimate event had been the biggest and most brutal but everyone had been told that this year's last event would be the biggest ever. The anticipation was incredible. In the second last event, twenty men had taken part. Each was given four throwing daggers and they were told to spread out in a large circle. The crowd had spread out even wider and what had taken place was almost like a game of modern day dodge-ball where kids run around throwing the ball at each other and if you are hit, you are out. The main difference was that the ball had been replaced with knives and if you were hit you were more than likely very badly injured, dying or dead. Seven people in the crowd had been hit with knives, two of them dying. No one in the crowd seemed overly fussed about the deaths and very few had taken their eyes off the show for more than a few seconds. As the last man standing pulled a knife from his right arm he was surrounded by four of the best looking girls from the Braided Pony and helped inside where his wounds would be tended to before he had things done to him that he had never imagined.

Even before the women had started to lead him off the entire crowd's eyes had already turned to Stan. Stan got to his feet and got back on top of his table. "Can I assume everyone has enjoyed the show?" The alcohol fuelled rabble went into the biggest uproar yet. Drinks were thrown, almost every man there with a gun fired into the air, hats were tossed, fights broke out. As Stan looked around the rabble, the sun dipped behind the horizon. Stan began to speak again, "You were all promised our biggest event ever this year. Well, I am a man of my word and I very rarely disappoint, so, without further ado, I give you the first ever vampire in captivity! Valery!!" Stan roared the vampire's name, as he watched the cage being drawn out from behind the Braided Pony. Four of Stan's goons, just having brought it up from the cellar and dragged it round front on a small cart. The crowd looked on in awe. Not one person laughed, the woman looked too unearthly, like a living statue. She was completely naked and her skin was chalk-white. The light from the oil lanterns bounced off her sleek muscles, that looked more defined than most of the men's in the crowd. She held onto two of the front bars and surveyed the crowd but did not move. A shiver ran down the spines of several of the bystanders and for the first time ever some of the spectators started to leave, heading for home. While the crowd thinned out it by no means disappeared. Some stepped in closer, filling the gaps left by those who had left.

"For our last event of the evening, I will turn over ten percent of the Braided Pony's earnings for an entire year to any man who can go into the cage and last thirty seconds and come back out again. Everyone in the crowd knew this was more than they could hope to make in a few years never mind one but they also knew just by looking at the thing in the cage that it was unlikely to be an easy feat. There was something feline and predatory about her even though she stood stock-still.

"I'll do it!" came from near the front of the crowd.

"Who is our first brave contestant?" Stan shouted above the murmurs that broke out.

One of the younger revellers pushed his way out of the crowd and positioned himself in front of Stan.

"Well, well. Why don't you introduce yourself to everyone son." Stan said.

"My name is Tommy Branigan and I can last thirty seconds with that woman!"

The crowd cheered and applauded at a mixture of his bravery and wanting to see anyone in the cage just to see what happened. Most of them would have been impressed enough to see a real live vampire but the thought of seeing someone in the cage with her had both their curiosities and blood lust going.

Tommy had appeared in town only months earlier with a young pregnant girl. They had kept themselves to themselves and Tommy had worked various jobs since arriving so people generally liked him. He was a big lad for twenty years old and not so quick of wit.

"The money will buy some land for my family and set us up for life." He told the crowd, although no one was particularly interested in what he would do if he survived the next few minutes.

"Okay son, let's get started," Stan said, then jumped down from the table he stood on and started walking Tommy to the cage with his hand on his back. The woman in the cage didn't even turn towards them as they stepped up next to her. Stan's goons moved in closer brandishing well- lit torches and quickly thrust them at the front of the cage. The vampire inside stepped back slowly, not making a sound and kept her eyes on the cage door. Stan could feel Tommy start to shake through his jacket.

"You'll be okay son, just keep moving." Stan said, having no real idea what would happen. The vampire had barely moved since they captured her. She hadn't fought or tried to escape. They had managed to capture her in the daytime when she was at her weakest but she had been in the basement of the bar for 6 days now and no trouble so far. Stan just hoped that having a live victim in close proximity would be enough to send her into a fit of rage. Especially since she hadn't eaten in days, though he had no idea how often she needed to eat. She stayed where she was at the back of the cage as two men stood at either side and the other two approached the cage door. Stan gave Tommy a little push on the back so he would step forward and onto the trailer. The crowd was absolutely silent. Tommy stepped up to the door and with all four men holding their torches close, the cage door was opened and, with a little nudge, Tommy stepped in.

The vampire didn't move. Neither did Tommy. Both stood at opposite ends of the cage staring into each other's eyes. Valery's eyes, were like cat's eyes. Tommy could feel his heart beating in his chest as he looked her over. She was beautiful in a terrifying sort of way. Much better looking than any of the girls in the Braided Pony but Tommy could feel his flesh crawling. The crowd looked on in silence. Everyone expected the vampire to attack him as soon as he entered the cage but she just stood where she was.

Stan nodded to the goons surrounding the cage and they stepped in and thrust their torches through the bars, hitting Valery in the back. In the beat of a heart she grabbed both torches and pulled them from the hands of the men outside the cage. Tommy took a quick step backwards, his back colliding with the now locked cage door. The vampire looked down at the torches in her hands and smiled before throwing them through the bars, towards the crowd. For the first time since she appeared the crowd made some noise. There were screams from those who tried to get out of the way of the lit, flying torches and even louder shrieks of pain from those they hit. Stan was at a loss as to what he should do. He knew the crowd would not be happy with this show so he stepped closer to Tommy and told him he would up the prize to twenty percent of the year's takings but he had to attack Valery and give them a show. Stan had no intention of paying the man anything and doubted he would survive the ordeal. Tommy on the other hand had no intention of attacking the woman before him and was beginning to wonder why he volunteered in the first place. He couldn't provide for his family if he was dead.

The crowd started to hiss and boo due to the lack of action. Patience was not a virtue of the town's people. Some of the crowd began to throw food at Stan and his goons. Nothing like this had ever occurred at any of the previous games days and Stan knew that things could turn nasty real quick. He was a respected and feared person in the town but no man could win over an angry mob. Fearing for what may happen if things got too out of control, Stan jumped up onto the cart that the cage sat on and fished the keys out of his pocket. Two of his henchmen hopped up next to him as expected and pointed their shotguns through the bars, aimed at the female vampire. Stan slipped the key into the lock. Very few people in the crowd noticed the vampire's fingers stretch and thicken as they became more talon like. Before any human ear could hear the click as the key opened the lock Valery slammed into the bars of the cage door. The speed and force of her passing had flung Tommy aside as the cage door flew open, throwing Stan and his boys into the crowd. No human eye was fast enough to follow her as she moved through the three- hundred- strong crowd. As one man looked down to see his guts slide out of his torn-open stomach, she had removed the heads of four more, while tearing the hearts from others. The crowd didn't have time to scatter—never mind escape. Valery killed without prejudice, man woman and child. Her victims were plentiful and deserving. There was no family in the town that deserved mercy in her eyes. It was a town of criminals. Something was rotten in the earth and it drew the wrong sort of person. She could feel the blackness rising off of everyone, even more from the ones she tasted as she ripped out their throats. The only truly decent person for hundreds of miles was Tommy. She had felt it as soon as he had stepped out of the crowd. He was a good man, a deserving man, a man who only wanted to do right and knew no wrong. An indecent thought had never crossed his mind. She had lived for centuries, looking for an equal, looking for someone who was as true in soul as herself. The 'dark gift', as she called it, could bring the end of mankind. In the hands of the wrong person it could be used to destroy everything. Not one person she had encountered on any continent had ever come close to having as bright an aura as Tommy. She would turn him, she would make him her own. They would take over the Braided Pony and build a new town: a town for good people—a town for those who wanted to be good and do good— and those who came to town with evil on their minds would be dealt with swiftly.

Valery stood naked, whilst she surveyed the carnage around her.

Tommy was the only person left alive, cowering in his cage. He would be okay once she brought him over. She knew that through time he would see that there was no other way.

Thirteen Voices

By

Kevin J. Kennedy

As far back as I can remember, I always had voices in my head. When I was around five it just seemed like thoughts, but by the time I was seven I knew they weren't my own... They had become louder, more distinct and they argued. I didn't even understand what they were talking about sometimes. They never caused me any trouble. They didn't try to get me to do things and they weren't evil, like most of the voices people seem to have in their heads in fiction. My voices were just kind of there, annoying and sometimes they made it hard to concentrate, but there wasn't much I could do about it. I never told anyone, especially my parents. I watched enough television to know that I would just end up sitting in some doctor's room being asked moronic questions. I tried talking to the voices a few times, but they never answered and I was never mentioned in any of their conversations.

There were quite a lot of them. Twelve, I think, but there would only ever be two or three conversing at any given time and sometimes it would be quiet for ages. It was as if my head was a room and I could only hear the conversations when people entered it. That's probably the best way I can describe it. Sometimes they were there and sometimes they weren't. The voices changed and different voices seemed to talk about different things. It could all get confusing, but I mainly tried to just ignore them. As we couldn't communicate with each other there really wasn't much else for it.

On the day of my thirteenth birthday I heard a new voice. At first I didn't notice because I was busy and was pushing the voices to the back of my head. Then I realised it just kept saying, *'hey you.'* It would say it and wait a few seconds and then say it again, but no one was responding. I stopped what I was doing and concentrated. The voice became louder as I focused on it more.

'Hey you.'

'Are you talking to me?' I asked the voice in my head.

'Who else?' it responded.

'You can hear me?'

'I'm answering you, aren't I?'

All those years with the voices and now all of a sudden one of them was talking to me. I felt a little dizzy. I can remember sitting down on the curb and as soon as my butt hit the concrete the voice was at it again.

'Now that you are comfy, do you think we could get to business?'

'Business?' I asked it.

'Yes, business. Planning what we do next. We need to work together.'

'Work together?'

'Jesus Christ, kid. Are you going to repeat everything I say? You got brain damage or something?'

'I'm beginning to wonder.'

'Funny. I like it. You and I will get along just fine. Now, where do we get laid around here?'

'Laid?'

'Seriously? Everything I say? You sure you're not slow?'

'I'm finding this all a little hard to take in. I've always had voices in my head, but they have never spoken to me before.'

'Consider me special. Now, where were we on getting laid?'

'I can't get laid. I'm only thirteen and that's only from today. It's my birthday.'

'Happy birthday, kid. What about a hooker? They don't care if you're thirteen.'

'I can't get a hooker.'

'Stripper and pay her a little extra?'

'No hookers and no strippers.'

'Okay. It's your birthday. Let's just get fucked up instead.'

'I'm not getting fucked up, there will be no hookers and no strippers.'

'Man, this is going to be a dull ride. I'm sorry about this, kid, but I'm gonna have to take over for a bit.

'Take over?'

'Wow, you can't help yourself. Look, it's like this: I borrowed an amulet from this old lady in

Hades. I hadn't been there all that long, but it's not a particularly nice place to visit if you know what I mean. I saw a chance and I took it. You'd have done the same.'

'Borrowed or stole?'

'You really are a soft touch, kid.'

'Tell me.'

'Well, I stole it but I don't see what difference it makes. I'm going to borrow your body for a little while and then you can have it back.'

'Borrow, like the type of borrowing you did with the old lady? Are either her or me likely to get these borrowed items back?'

'Look, kid. It's not like you have a say in the matter, but yes, she will get her amulet back and you will get your body back. I'm sure a party has already been dispatched from Hades to bring me back. I'll

probably have your body for six hours, maximum, maybe even less.'

'So you are just going to take my body and I get no say, and then I get it back at some undetermined time?'

'You make it sound so wrong. I get to live a little and you get to have a nice rest. When you wake up, you might not even be a virgin anymore?'

'What? You can't? I... It's my body and I should be the one to do that.'

'Just relax, kid. You will be back in charge before you know it.'

And that was it—lights out. I didn't go to the back of the brain and still have an idea of what was going on. It was complete darkness. No, less than that. Complete nothingness. No feeling of time or anything. I was in my body and then I wasn't, and then I was back again. It was a bit like blacking out for just a second.

The moment I was back in my body I knew something was wrong, though. My body felt bigger, heavier and stiffer. I found it harder to breath. It took about twenty seconds before my sight came back. I was in a communal room in what appeared to be an old folk's home. There were old people sitting in comfy chairs everywhere. The walls were draped in banners for a birthday party. 'Happy 73rd' they read.

I looked down at my body. I was wearing striped pyjamas and a bathrobe. There was a piece of card sticking out of my pocket. I pulled it out.

It read: Listen kid, I'm sorry. I know I had your body a little longer than we both thought, but you know how it is. I'm sure you've still got a few good years left in that body. If it's any consolation, you're not a virgin anymore. I had been close to getting caught for a while now, so I thought I'd give myself up on your birthday and let you enjoy your day. It's my fault you've missed them all since we became acquainted on your thirteenth, after all. I'm not a completely bad guy. If I break back out of Hell anytime soon and you are still alive, I'll pay you a visit in my new body and we can have a beer. Happy seventy- third, kid!

The End

Don't Grass

By

Kevin J. Kennedy

Day 1

Andrew knew that his first day of school was going to be a nightmare. He had been picked on in his old school, and being the new guy in a new school at the age of fifteen wasn't going to be easy. He knew he stood out like a sore thumb. His uniform was too small for him last year, and after his growth spurt over the summer holidays, he was ready to burst out of it. His no-longer-white school shirt was stretched tight over his skin, and the buttons were ready to burst. His grey school trousers were too short, and the soles of his shoes were hanging off. Not exactly the kind of first impression he wanted to make, but he had little choice.

His mother had been drinking heavily ever since his father left and was showing no signs of making a change. Andrew had been working a paper route in the mornings and a few cash- in- hand shifts in the local chip shop in the evenings. Since they had been evicted from their last place and had to move, he could no longer do either job as they were just too far away. Not only did he have to start a new school and worry about how he would be treated, but he was worried about getting a new job or two as his mother would quickly drink away the benefit money she received.

Before leaving for school, Andrew peeked his head into his mother's room. She wasn't there. When he walked along the hall to the living room, he found her half on and half off the couch. He quickly lifted her legs onto the couch and covered her with a throw from the chair. An empty bottle of vodka lay next to her. He knew it had been unopened yesterday, so she had drunk the entire bottle in a day. Her habit was getting worse. It was now a rare occasion when she would be in any sort of sober state.

Grabbing his worn school bag, Andrew left quickly and began his walk to school. His mind swam with a million worries. Would his mum ever get better? Would he get a job? Would they lose another home? Would he be picked on at this school as well as the last?

As he walked towards the school in a daze, he never heard the group of lads across the road shouting at him.

"Haw you! Haw you, am fuckin' talkin tae ye!"

No sooner had the voices registered in his head than he was grabbed from the side and rushed into the wall behind him. It took a second before he realised a much larger boy had him pinned to the wall, holding him up by the front, off his feet so he had to stand on his tip toes.

The boy who was holding Andrew against the wall was Barry Brown. He was a hulk of a lad but not just because of his genetics; he had been held back in school for two years, so he was naturally much bigger than the others he hung around with. Andrew noticed while looking at him that his brow was really low and prominent, and his eyes were a little too close together. It gave him a look of one of the inbred monsters that eat people in horror movies. The bright ginger hair and mass of freckles that covered his face did nothing to improve his looks.

"A fuckin' shouted on you, ya wee dick. Did ye no hear me?" Barry asked Andrew.

Andrew having dealt with multiple bullies in his time knew that his answer was irrelevant. If he had been chosen by the bully to be picked on, the outcome had already been decided. Nonetheless, he knew he had to try something.

"I'm new here. No one knows me. I kinda heard someone shouting, but I didn't think it would be me they were shouting on."

"Aw, ye didny think, did ye no? Well, when a fucking shout on ye, ye answer me!"

Again, Andrew knew that whether he answered or not, it would likely make no difference but felt it best to answer.

"Okay, sorry. I didn't realise."

As Andrew finished his sentence he felt a fist crash into his jaw. It was a solid punch and knocked him sideways. He tripped over his own feet and landed on the ground. Knowing that this was normally enough for the bully to prove their dominance and get a laugh out of their friends, he assumed it would be over, but just as he heard the group that surrounded Barry laughing, he felt a foot crash into his stomach and the air rush out of him. His eyes filled with water as he struggled to draw air.

As he began to be able to breathe again, he could see the feet of the group walking away, and he heard Barry call over his shoulder, "Ye better no fuckin' grass on us, ya wee dick."

Day 2

When Andrew woke up on the morning of his second day of school, he was filled with much more dread than the day before. While nothing else had happened to him the previous day, he had spent the entire day at school trying to avoid people who may have been part of the group who attacked him, but he had only really looked at Barry, so everyone he saw could have been one of the others. It made for a long- drawn- out worrying experience. By the time he got home, he had been exhausted and fell straight asleep. He had woken back up at 11pm and hadn't been able to get back to sleep all night. He had finally fallen asleep at five thirty in the morning only to be woken an hour and a half later when his alarm went off. He just hoped that yesterday was a clear-cut case of people picking on the new guy and that for the rest of the year he would fly below the radar. He planned on leaving school at the end of the year anyway to get a job and look after his mother.

While putting on his too-small clothes, Andrew wondered if he had been picked at random, because of his clothes, or because he was a new face. He also knew it could be none of these things and just a chance occurrence. Bullies were funny like that. They would pick on anyone if the timing was right and they thought it would get a laugh. Andrew understood that being tall and skinny, and wearing old clothes made him stand out.

When Andrew found his mother in the same position as yesterday, with a new bottle of vodka almost empty by her side, he decided to leave her as she was. She wasn't helping him with his life, so why should he help her? As he shut the door behind him, he felt angry at the hand he had been dealt. Ideas ran through his head about what he would do if the any bullies came near him again, how he would unleash his anger and make sure they knew he wasn't someone to be messed with.

"Haw, c'mere!"

The shout came from across the street. Andrew knew instantly that it was the same voice that had shouted at him yesterday. His mind started racing with options: he could run, he could keep walking and ignore them, and if they approached him, he could show them he wasn't to be trifled with. Or he could go to them as requested and hope that the worse he got was a group of people he didn't know making fun of him and laughing at him. None of the considered options bothered him much. While he knew that going to them could end in disaster, it seemed like the safest option considering he would be at school with them all day, every day, and probably find it impossible to avoid them for a full year. Every thought had raced through his mind in a matter of a second, and though he made his decision quickly, a shout came as he began to turn around.

"Haw, a thought a fuckin' told you yesterday, when a shout, you..."

Barry cut his sentence short as he saw Andrew turn and begin to walk towards them. For a split-second, Andrew thought he saw a flicker of hesitation in Barry's eyes, but it was gone before he could be sure. Andrew quickly crossed the road and made his way towards them, terrified at the prospect of what would happen to him, but too scared to do anything else.

Yesterday Andrew had had no time to see his attackers coming., Today, as he crossed the road and walked towards them, he had the presence of mind—terrified as he was—to look them over as he approached, so he would know who to avoid in school. There were a few of them, but there seemed to be four that were clearly at the front and were smiling at his approach. There were two small lads that were either a year or two below or were tiny for their age. They were obviously identical twins, and their size had no bearing on their menace. They stood up front next to Barry, and both had evil grins spread across their face. Next to Barry and the twins stood a short fat girl. She looked like the living incarnation of Miss Piggy from the Muppets. Ugly was an understatement. She looked like she had been dressed by Andrew's mother. Her skirt barely covered the crotch of her knickers, and her shirt looked like it was closer to bursting than Andrew's was, her belly fat stretching it more than her bosom did.

"A thought a told ye yesterday, that when a shout you answer quickly."

"I came over as soon as I heard you," Andrew answered, knowing it was the wrong thing to say as soon as it came out of his mouth.

He was quickly proven correct when he felt a punch connect with his jaw once again. The punch carried none of the force of the one from the day before that took him off of his feet, but it was painful all the same. He knew it was a warning punch to keep him in his place.

"You talkin' back, ya wee dick?" Barry asked, but Andrew knew it wasn't a question.

While his mind raced as to whether his best defence would be to answer, apologise, or run, he was hit with an open- handed slap.

"You slow or something, lanky?" he was asked.

"No... I..." Andrew tried to respond. His years of bullying did nothing to make his mind work quick enough to outsmart the bullies.

"A fink he is a dummy," the fat lass, who was called Madona, said. Her mother was so wasted when she filled in the birth certificate, she couldn't even spell 'Madonna' properly.

Andrew turned his attention towards her, looked her over, and knew exactly who she was in a split second. As he focused back on Barry, the twins were stepping up to either side of him, pressing in against him. People getting into his personal space had always riled his temper, not that he could do anything. The odds were against him. Besides, he had never thrown a punch in his life. It was easier just to take it. He figured that throwing two quick elbows would probably put both of the twins with wee-man syndrome on their asses, shouting for their mummy, but he was in no position to find out.

As his mind wandered, like always, he felt the next punch land, right in the stomach. He doubled over before falling to his knees.

"Gies yer money, or yer getting battered," Barry told him.

Andrew knew that giving over the seventy pence that was in his pocket was probably not going to save him. Most bullies expected more. However, some wanted just to hurt you and giving them the cash only angered them as you took away their only excuse to hit you, so you would end up getting it worse for complying. Andrew decided to give it a try and pulled the coins from his pocket and held them out. One of the twins slapped the coins from his hand and hit him in the face. It was one of the weakest punches Andrew had ever felt in all his years of dealing with bullies, but he kept his mouth shut. When it all came down to it, a soft hit was a win in his books. It was followed by an equally pansy punch from the other twin.

Leaving the money lying where it fell, and Andrew on his knees, the entire group turned and walked away.

"Ye better no fuckin' grass on us, ya cunt!" the Miss Piggy look-alike shouted to him as they walked away.

Day 3

There was going to be no way that Andrew was getting to school without meeting his new tormentors. There was only one way to the school from where he lived, and he knew they would be waiting for him. He toyed with the idea of going in late, but he knew the school would contact his mother, and in her current state, that was a massive no-no. He had gone back and forth over his options through most of the night. Like the night before, he had very little sleep and it was wearing on him. He only wished that he could talk things over with his mother and get some advice, but she would probably just tell him it didn't matter and try and get him to take a drink. It wouldn't be the first time she tried to help him with his problems by offering him some alcohol.

He got ready and left for school like the days before, but he felt angrier than he ever had. He knew there had to be something he could do. Most of the anger was directed towards himself, even though he knew that it was unlikely that there was much he could do to improve his situation. Telling his school would result in a two- to three-day break from bullying, then it would become worse. Telling his mother would prove useless. He had no friends to tell. It was a situation with a no- win in sight, and it frustrated him beyond belief. Andrew didn't think he had a bad bone in his body, but some days he wished that he could just make the people who tormented him disappear. He didn't want to hurt them as much as just make them vanish from existence.

As he approached the first set of steps on the hill that took people up from the rest of the scheme to the high-rise flats, his body tensed. There were four sets of steps that led up from the scheme to the twenty-four-story high-rise flat. It stood on a huge hill that the entire housing estate encircled, but the hill in the middle was massive. The four sets of stairs had twenty-four stairs each before you got to the ground level of the tower block that led you to the front entrance. There was no other way up apart from walking up the steep grassy banks. The gang that tormented Andrew seemed to hold fort on the bottom few stairs. He arrived in front of them, his body shaking in fear this time. He knew there would be a punishment for doing no more than minding his own business.

"You trying to take the piss, wee man?" one of the tiny twins asked. The 'wee man' comment was ironic, as Andrew was positive he could knee them both in the face without much effort, but wee man or not, there was a team of them, and it rendered him helpless. Inbred Barry couldn't have smiled wider if he had tried. Andrew wanted nothing more than to smash his face in but knew it would never happen. Somewhere in the back of his brain, he was telling himself to stand up for once, but he knew it was the wrong move. Before his mind could take control of his body and brain, his fear took over and put him into autopilot.

"Are you acting hard because you have wee-man-syndrome or because you are scared of your pal?" Andrew asked the twin who had spoken. His entire body tightened as the words came out of his mouth.

Within a split second, the twins attacked him, simultaneously. It was like being attacked by a group of small children. Each blow was laughable, but Andrew felt the need to act like they hurt because an attack from their leader would no doubt cause a considerable amount of pain. In the hope that the top boy wouldn't step in, Andrew dropped to the ground in the pretence that the twins had somehow knocked him down. He assumed that this would bring a swift end to this day's torment, but he was sorely wrong. Barry the Prick, as Andrew had now come to think of him, had put his size eleven boot right on Andrews chest. He rested his weight on the foot and pinned Andrew to the ground. Andrew tried with all his might to get out from under the boot as he could feel that something much worse than the twins' pitiful beating was coming. He had made a mistake submitting, and he was going to pay for it. He could feel it in his bones.

Miss Piggy, the group's only girl, was the girl who had been passed around to each of them—who had wanted to be one of them so badly, but knew they just used her—was filled with more hatred than most of the others. She was arguably the evillest of them all but spent most of her life being a piece of meat for the gang. Her free time was spent taking her hatred out on anyone she could. When the gang allowed her to step up, she tried to show them she was as tough as anyone else in the group. They didn't care. She would always be the fat slut that let them do what they wanted. She was just another victim, but she was on the inside, and Andrew wasn't.

Andrew lay on the ground, hoping that the pitiful attack that the twins gave him would end it. He assumed by their stance and way of acting that they were held in high regard by the group, but he had no idea of what was to come. As he lay, pinned to the ground by the inbreed's large boot, he watched as each of the group lit their lighters and held them on their side to heat the metal. He started thrashing around under the foot as he realised what was coming. Miss Piggy leaned forward and ripped his shirt open. There was an evil grin on her face as she stood back up, smiling down at Andrew. As his eyes scanned the group, even in his fear-stricken state he noticed that everyone was moving back apart from the main four tormentors. Just as the thought entered his brain, he felt the metal rim of all four lighters pressed into his chest. He couldn't see straight enough as it went on to see the rest of the group scatter. His nostrils filled with the scent of burnt flesh and hair as the few hairs on his chest were burnt off and his skin was scarred.

As the group walked away laughing, leaving Andrew lying on the ground with his chest feeling like it was on fire, he rolled onto his side and wished he was dead.

"Remember, nae fuckin' grassin, bawbag," one of the group shouted.

He lay there for a long time, until it began to rain, and still he didn't move. The heavier the rain poured from the sky, the more it soothed his chest and cooled his skin, and yet, the warmer Andrew began to feel. The rage that built inside him was enough to make his skin boil. He was torn between two worlds. In reality, he knew he was the lone animal in the wilderness that was an easy meal for predators, but a small part of his brain told him that he was wrong, that he was playing possum, that he could be bigger than any of the bullies that tormented him. He knew if the circumstances were right that he could be victorious, and then the rain stopped. His chest began to burn again, and he knew his brain was leading him astray. He was a victim. He would always be a victim. It was his role in life. Why else would he walk the path he walked?

Day 4

On the last school day of the week, Andrew knew he should feel happy. He had four days off in a row, just around the corner. It was a long weekend, and he knew he didn't need to leave the house, other than to maybe run to the store for some groceries. He could avoid every bully in the world if he planned it right. Just one more day to get through, but Andrew hadn't made it to his new school once without being attacked and assaulted in one way or another. The burns on his chest were agony, and they looked like they may get infected, but he couldn't tell his mother or the school for fear of repercussions, so he would just have to ride it out and hope for the best.

Wearing the same too-small clothes that hadn't been washed in a while, he left his new home once again. As much as he was in pain the night before, he had toyed with the idea of wandering the tract of houses hoping to find a different route to school, but aside from the fact he didn't feel like doing anything apart from lying in bed with a can of his mum's lager on his chest to cool the pain, he was scared if he went outside that he would run into the gang somewhere else. He knew they frequented the bottom of the high-rise stairs in the mornings, but he had no idea where they hung around in the evenings.

It was another night of little sleep, and when he did wake up in the morning, he felt off balance. His chest was agony, and he had barely slept in days. He ate very little due to having no money coming in from any jobs anymore and his mother spending every penny she got from benefits on alcohol.

Putting his school shirt on was a nightmare, and as much as it embarrassed him, he ended up using one of his mother's sanitary towels as a bandage to keep the material of the shirt from pressing against his chest.

After the struggle of getting dressed, he checked his mother's room as usual in the hope that he would find her in bed, even if she was passed out drunk. It would be a good sign that she had made it to bed before passing out in a drunken stupor. As always, the bed hadn't been slept in. On walking down the hall, Andrew found his mother fully on the floor this time. There were no vodka bottles. She was running out of money. There were two, three litre bottles of strong, cheap cider lying empty on either side of her. Andrew stood and looked at her for a few minutes to see if she would move. The time passed quickly as he didn't focus on her. He knew she wouldn't move. He barely ever saw her in any alert state anymore, and he knew she had stopped caring about him a while ago. She no longer spoke to him and had proven that her only interest was in how she felt. The nasty things she said aside, her actions proved her to be nothing but a cunt. Andrew no longer felt any connection to her. In their old home, things were bad, but her actions alone had brought them to their current state of affairs. As he was about to turn and leave as usual, something in his brain clicked. He turned back and stood over his mother. He looked down at her with nothing but disgust in his heart. Hocking it from the back of his throat, Andrew pulled a green phlegmy glob of spit into his mouth and spat on his mother's face. She didn't so much as flicker an eyelid, passed out in a drunken coma. As he turned on his heels and left, Andrew knew he wouldn't care if his mother died that day. The more he thought about it, he wasn't too bothered if he died either.

Deciding that looking for a new route was pointless, he started off on the same path he took each day. As he got closer to the stairs that led up the hill to the bottom of the high-rise flats, he couldn't help but think about how intimidating they were. The flats looked old and worn and the cladding was stained black in most parts. The height of the block alone was scary to look up at, but the fact that it sat on top of a sizeable hill in the middle of the otherwise flat scheme added to its menace. It seemed like a perfect place for a group of assholes to live. He wasn't even sure if they all lived in the high rise or if it was just a place to hang out. He could see the group from a good distance. As always, there were loads of them. He knew bullies always travelled in packs. They needed someone else to find them funny when they were tormenting someone, but he knew that the numbers intimidated most. He wondered if they would act so hard on their own, but decided it was a wasted thought as he had never seen any of them on their own, not even in school. They were all as dumb as each other and they were all in the bottom classes together—even Barry who had had two years more than everyone else to learn the work, but it only proved how much of a waster he was.

Stopping in his tracks, Andrew wondered whether he should go on. There was no part of him that wanted to experience another run-in with the bullies, but there was no way to get past them. He had thought about waiting until they had gone to school, but he knew they got in late every day, so he would need to go in even later, and then he would get into trouble from the teachers or headmaster. Being the new boy in school, he knew they would be keeping a close eye on him. He knew he had no options. He would just need to hope that after yesterday's attack, they would leave him alone now. He still couldn't believe they had actually burned him. He couldn't imagine they would go any further. They were kids as well after all. Deciding it was best to get whatever was going to happen over with, he started a quick march along the street, staying on the opposite side of the street.

The other days the gang had shouted at him or came up from behind him after he passed by. Today he saw them begin to cross the street towards him before he was even near them. He decided to just keep walking.

"You no learned yer lesson yet?" came a shout.

Andrew wanted to ask them what lesson. That people were naturally cunts? That a low IQ and possible inbreeding meant you had to lash out at the world? That scum would be better off being put down at birth? There were a multitude of things he could think of, but none of them were a lesson. He knew guys like Barry and his gang before he moved to his new home. They gravitated towards the weak and lost, and Andrew considered himself to be both.

"A fuckin' asked you a question! You've obviously no learned."

Andrew expected Barry to step forward and attack him, but this time Miss Piggy lurched forward and drew both her hands down his face in a claw-like fashion, her nails tearing the skin as she went. Andrew let out a scream that started the gang laughing before they began to mimic him. His hands quickly rose to his torn face, but that just made the pain worse.

"Awww," Miss Piggy taunted, before she began raining blows on Andrew's face. Her punches were weak, but when they hit the freshly torn skin, it was painful. A few blows landed on the ridges of his face, and those hurt too. Once again, Andrew ended up on the ground. Hitting the ground seemed to be a signal for the jackals to attack and the kicks began to rain in. He had no idea how many people were kicking him, but there were feet coming from all directions. The assault was quick but brutal. He thought he heard someone shouting at the gang to leave him alone, but he couldn't be sure. When they left him lying on the ground, no one came to his aid.

Getting up, Andrew realised that his shirt and his trousers were torn. He couldn't go into school in the state he was in. He was going to have to go home and face the music. The uniform wasn't only ripped, but it was more filthy than usual, so he knew he wouldn't be able to fly below the radar. As he was about to head back home, he heard a shout come from the distance.

"Ye better no fuckin' grass."

Andrew began his walk home, filled with dread at the notion of asking his mother for some new clothes.

Day 5

Andrew had lain awake until six o'clock in the morning before he had finally nodded off. His body and face were racked with pain, and his mind would not slow down. He had slept for an entire forty-five minutes before waking up feeling worse than he did before he fell asleep. He had been unable to wake his mother up when he got home, and by the time he heard her rouse, he had lost the confidence to talk to her. At first, he thought he would hide out until he heard her start to drink again and try and time it for when she would be at her merry stage. Unfortunately, he had spent so long avoiding her, he no longer knew how long after starting that stage kicked in, or if his mother even went through the merry stage anymore. She was just an angry drunk these days as far as he knew. He then began to think about trying to catch her just before she was at the passing out stage and if she would maybe give him money for clothes, not really knowing what she was doing. He doubted there was any money left, and he couldn't really convince himself to believe there was a best time to ask for the clothes he now needed.

On awakening, the fear of the situation he was in outweighed the pain he felt, and he was in a lot of pain. The worry about the bullies seemed a distant second to the worry about dealing with his mother. He passed them once each day, but he lived with his mother, and she could hurt him every minute she was awake. He knew what she was capable of when she lost control. The stress was worse than the pain. The more the thoughts swirled in his mind, the angrier he felt. In his old home, he knew who to avoid and how to avoid them. Here, he felt like he was trapped. He felt like someone was standing on his chest. No amount of thought or preparation was going to help him. He was now in a living nightmare where the only future in sight was likely to get worse day by day. He didn't know how many more beatings he could take or if he would survive much more. How far would his bullies go? Would they get to the stage where each day was a new endangerment of his life? Was there any point in going on? Who would care if he was gone?

Andrew cried, and he cried hard. He hadn't cried since he was a toddler. He wasn't tough physically, but he was tough mentally, or at least he used to be. He got up from his bed and opened his bedroom door. He walked along the hall and went into the bathroom. He got one of his mother's cheap BIC razors and broke it in the sink. He picked up the loose blade that had separated from the plastic and he slid it across his wrist. He didn't cut deep, and he cut horizontally rather than vertically. He knew it shouldn't kill him, but he wanted to feel the pain, and a large part of him wanted to risk it. When the blood started to pour, his face went chalk white. He grabbed a towel and pushed it hard against the cut. There were no medical supplies, but after a while he managed to get the blood to slow, and he used an old t-shirt and some masking tape to make a makeshift bandage. He sat on his bed and looked at it for a while. He wondered why he felt nothing. He was pretty sure that's where he was, in a valley of feeling of nothing, but the longer he looked at his wound, the more the rage crept back. He wondered if there was anything that he wasn't angry at. He couldn't think of anything. He hated his life, he hated life in general. What was the fucking point?

For the next four hours, Andrew sat on the edge of his bed. He never moved a muscle. Various pains cried out all over his body, but he never let them register much. At one point he heard his mother get up, stagger about, and then an almighty crash. Everything was silent after that. He hoped that she had smashed her head open and had bled out on the floor. Fuck her. Parents were supposed to care. Parents were supposed to look after you. The more Andrew thought about it, no one seemed to follow the rules. He wondered why he did. There was not a single person that he could bring to mind that followed the rules we were all meant to follow other than himself. The thought helped to add fuel to the fire. Andrew thought about killing his mother. If the idea of her being dead made him feel happy, then why shouldn't he just end her life? It would be easy. She was a fucking vegetable most of the day and night. He didn't believe he could do it, though. He still had fond memories of his younger years with her. The bullies, however, he felt nothing for but resentment. The bullies he could hurt. He wondered to himself if he could really hurt someone, and he laughed out loud, going into fits of laughter. Hysterical, he fell off the side of his bed, crashing onto the floor and hurting every cut, bruise, scratch, and slash on his body. It only furthered his hysterics. As the pain shot through his body, he laughed harder. It was a while before he calmed down and lay staring at the ceiling. The pain enveloped him, but it felt different. He embraced it. It was different from the pain he felt in his mind every day. It was real. He could make sense of it. Sitting up, he smiled. It felt good. Having something to smile for made it feel well-earned and worthwhile.

As Andrew left the house, the grin was still spread across his face. He wore the same old tattered school uniform he wore ever day. The fact that there was no school made no difference. The ripped, smelly uniform was still in a better state than the other clothes he owned. The only change to the uniform was that his rucksack with books had been left at home. In it's place, he carried an old Nike sports bag. It was for carrying jogging shoes or football boots. It had a draw string that pulled the top shut and doubled as the straps that went over your shoulders.

As Andrew walked the route he walked every morning, the grin remained firm on his face and there was a smile in his eyes for the first time in years. He got to the corner where he could see the stairs leading up the hill to the tower block, and his grin grew as he saw that the gang hung out there even on days that the school was off. He looked around him. His wide open, staring eyes locked onto a half brick. He walked over and crouched down, picked the brick up, and slipped it into the sports bag. He pulled the draw strings tight and slipped the bag over one shoulder. This time, as he walked towards the gang, he crossed the street towards them.

"Well, look who it is," someone called out. He didn't recognise the voice. There had to be over twenty of them today. The most he had thought there had been on the school days was ten or twelve. He stopped walking about twenty paces away from them.

"Fuck you doing here? You no learned your lesson yet?"

This time the voice came from Barry. Andrew knew he would have to say something. He was clearly their leader of sorts. Andrew stood entirely still. He said nothing. The gang looked between each other and laughed and joked.

"What the fuck you doing just standing there, freak?"

Barry's voice sounded different. Andrew could hear the loss of confidence.

"Am fuckin' talkin' tae you," Barry shouted, trying to sound authoritative.

Andrew didn't move. He could see Barry's pupils change from where he stood. He felt the change in the bully from where he stood. The hangers- on were too dumb to notice anything like that. A loud, shouty voice was enough to have them think that their leader was tough, but Andrew already knew that Barry was never challenged. His large stature had thrust him into a position of dominance that he didn't have the mental capacity to handle. Andrew was reasonably confident that with the new circumstances, he could maybe take Barry in a one-on-one fair fight, but that would never happen. Bullies hunted in packs. Every person there, boy or girl, would attack Andrew as soon as the first punch was swung.

Barry stared at Andrew with a level of rage that he had never felt before. No one challenged him. His brain struggled to cope as a new situation arose. Being a creature of habit was easy. Thinking on your feet when you were dumb as a board was difficult. Without any new thoughts entering his simple mind, Barry charged at Andrew with his crew a few steps behind him, ready to join in the beating of a lifetime.

Andrew didn't move. As Barry's lumbering form got to within a few steps of Andrew, Andrew took one step to the side while letting the sports bag slide off his shoulder. He caught the straps, allowed Barry two more steps, then swung the bag with all his might. He could feel the bone in Barry's face crumble through the bag straps as the half brick crushed his face. Barry hit the ground like a sack of sand with his eyes wide open. The team that had been running so fast behind him came to an abrupt stop and fell over each other trying to stay back from Andrew. Andrew stood stock still, looking down at his old tormentor. He looked at the gang, who were still slowly moving backwards, away from him, and then back to the ground. He wound the straps tighter in his hands so that only the bag was hanging free, and he flipped it over his shoulder. He smiled back at the gang and then began to systematically pulp the rest of Barry's face and skull. It was quick and brutal. Blood flew from the dead teens face in every angle. Bits of bone chipped off and hit his gang who lay on the ground or stood watching in total terror. Each of them with their mouth hanging wide open, unable to move from their spot. Finishing up, Andrew swung the bag back over his shoulder and turned his back on the gang. As he casually walked away, he began to whistle *The Gambler*. It had been his father's favourite song when he was alive. Stopping and thinking for a moment, he turned to face the former bullies, who hadn't moved and still stared at their former leader.

"Ye's better no fuckin grass by the way," Andrew said before turning and heading home to deal with his mother.

The End

Would You Sell Your Soul?

By

Kevin J Kennedy

Eric was one of the nicer trolls, probably the nicest if truth be known. He was one of very few trolls in the entire world who had moved into the big city amongst all the 'norms' as the other trolls called them. It had been a long time since trolls had come out of hiding but things hadn't changed all that much. Trolls were still looked down upon as a lower race although they had proven themselves to be as capable as humans, even more capable in some instances.

Trolls, unlike in books, weren't quite as Shrek-like as people thought. It was true that they were green and once upon a time they did eat children. But let's not kid ourselves, humanity has done some pretty brutal things as well yet we adapt and move on. Most trolls were between six- and seven- foot tall and although over ninety percent of them were varying shades of green, the odd purple troll could be found on occasion. They were all very well built but entirely in proportion. I've seen drawings of trolls where they are all upper body with little legs and arms and all sorts of other variations. In reality from the neck down trolls looked very similar to humans but looked like they had been on steroids from birth. Their faces aren't the prettiest, though, and they do slabber a lot.

Eric knew that he was pointed at and people spoke under their breath about him wherever he went. He would try his best not to pay attention, especially when passing the abusive people who called him names and spat at him. All his troll friends had told him it was stupid moving to the city but Eric had dreams of becoming the first famous troll author. He had been hunting in the woods when he was little and found a book. He hadn't known what it was so he had taken it back to the cave. None of the other trolls could read apart from his great granddaddy who had never learned to read himself but had been given the gift of reading and writing by an old magician in the form of a little potion he received as payment for a service he provided the magician.

It had turned out the story was about a little creature called a Hobbit. Eric had never heard of such a creature but he knew when he grew up he wanted to be an adventurer like the Hobbit. As the years passed and Eric read as many books as he could get a hold of, ideas of becoming an adventurer slipped away but other ideas arose. Eric would be an author, the first troll author. His granddaddy had spent a long time teaching him to read and write as it wasn't something that trolls had ever bothered with in the olden days, but he stuck with it and learned it well. He started writing his own tales that only his granddaddy could read, but on some nights the whole family would sit down together and he would read them to everyone.

More years passed and Eric was becoming a much more accomplished writer. He knew if he wanted to succeed in his dream he needed to move to the city and make some connections and get himself online. Writing stories in pencil in a cave was one thing but now he wanted to share his stories with the world. He packed his pig- skin suitcase with the bare necessities and set off on his journey to the dismay of his distraught mother.

It had taken a full week of walking to come down from his cave in the mountain and he had enjoyed every minute of the walk. This was his adventure. He slept under the stars and found several very comfy caves to rest in when the day became too warm. The good thing about being a troll was it was very rare that they felt cold and they ate most meats raw so there was no real need for constantly building camp fires. One particular section of the mountain had a dense forest that was heavily populated with his favourite flavour of squirrel so Eric spent an extra day there having a chill and smoking some of the fuzzleweed he had stolen from his granddaddy's pouch. Every time he had a smoke the hunger would kick in and he would suck all the yummy flesh right off a squirrel's bones as if he was eating a soft, succulent spare rib. Trolls had very strong teeth

When Eric came to the foot of the mountain and found himself at a main road, he just followed it until he found a small town. The town folks didn't really seem to mind Eric but they lived next to an area where there had been troll sightings years before the trolls actually came out so it was a little more open.

Over the next few weeks Eric took a few computer classes at the local library, set himself up with email, learned the basics on Word and found a list of publishers looking for stories. When he was little he had always made his granddaddy tell him scary stories as they were his favourite, so he looked at horror books first. He organised a place to stay in the big city, got himself set up with a job working in a recycling plant and sent off his first few stories to publishers.

When he got to the big city he noticed the coldness in others straight away. They didn't try to hide it. He wasn't welcome. He spent most of his time outside work hidden away in his apartment writing, which was what he wanted to do anyway. It took a while but emails started to come back with feedback on his stories: 'We really liked your story but it has to be darker,' 'We really liked your story but we're looking for something a little more graphic.'

Eric was very disappointed that his stories were rejected but it wasn't the worst feedback he could have received. He would just need to make his stories a little scarier. The only problem was that Eric was such a nice troll he didn't even like to hurt the characters in his book. Hearing a scary story of someone else's seemed somehow different. His own characters seemed more real to him and the thought of hurting them hurt his heart. He needed to speak to granddaddy so he set off on another adventure all the way back to the small town, through the woods, up the mountain and back to his cave.

His mother nearly knocked him over when she came barrelling out of the cave and jumped on him. When trolls are excited their saliva glands goes into over drive and by the time his mum let him go the back of his shirt was stuck to his back with her saliva. When everyone had came and seen him and asked him a million questions before leaving, he finally got some time alone with his great granddaddy.

"You're too soft, son. You've always been too soft."

"But I just like to be nice and keep everyone happy granddaddy."

"I know you do, son, but a long, long time ago trolls weren't friendly and we didn't want everyone to be happy. We terrorised villages and had campouts where humans were the food. The world's gone to pot."

"But granddaddy, everyone knows about us now so we have to fit in."

"People don't like change, son, and you've seen what it's like out there. Accepted with open arms were you?"

"Well. No."

"As I thought. Make a lot of friends did you?"

"Uh, Not really..."

"Son, I love you. In fact you are my favourite great- grand child but your kindness is your weakness. People and trolls alike have always tried to be something they are not. Maybe it's part of evolution or progress, or maybe it's because we are lead by the wrong people, but you cannot be an author writing grown- up stories for all to read with no life experience behind you at all. I read that every author puts a little piece of themselves into each story. Now I know you have read a lot of books and your head is full of ideas but now you need some practical experience. You want to write horror but I don't think you have done a bad deed in your life. It's time that changed."

That night Eric lay and thought about what his granddaddy had said. It seemed to make sense but he didn't really want to do something bad. On the other hand, he really, really wanted to be a successful author. Was it worth the sacrifice? He decided to sleep on it.

The next morning after a very peaceful sleep in the old cave Eric woke up feeling refreshed and knew what he had to do. He'd listen to granddaddy. He would be a very bad troll. Just for a little while, though. Just long enough to learn a few things to put in his stories and make them more believable.

Three years later...

Eric pulled up to his mock- Georgian mansion in his custom- built Ferrari. Walking inside he was surrounded by the smaller troll children in his family and dragged into the massive dining room where his mum was serving up a feast of various raw animals. He excused himself saying he wasn't feeling hungry and he had work to do. He made his way across the large foyer to his study, unlocked it and went inside. No one was allowed in his study. He started up his PC, poured himself a large whisky knowing his writing flowed easier with a little drink, and continued work on his third novel— the first two having been massive successes. He had certainly achieved his dream of being the first troll author. Not only was he the first, but he was currently outselling most human horror authors. And while he was hearing that authors were struggling, his entire family had never been so well off. Everyone was very proud of Eric and this gave him a great sense of achievement. The only problem was that he didn't sleep very well any more. He spent a lot of nights lying awake wondering if he had sold his soul to get what he wanted. He often reasoned he just did what needed to be done to get ahead. Eric closed his laptop having completed his work for the evening, poured himself another whisky and went to his safe. After typing in the code Eric reached inside and pulled out a reasonably fresh child's arm. He quickly ate all of the skin off the arm in strips as if eating a corn on the cob and then crunched through the bones before finishing his whisky. As Eric locked the safe he walked over to the large wall mirror and looked himself in the face. "That's the last one, Eric," he said to himself... but he knew it wasn't.

The End

Vampiro

By

Kevin J. Kennedy

They call me Vampiro. It's not my real name, but you tend to find that real names don't matter much when you join a carnival. Not a lot of time and effort went into picking a name for me. I was standing in a grungy little caravan and when they asked what my skills were, I told them I was a vampire. The old carnival owner that hired me had asked what that entailed.

"Drinking blood," I told him.

"Drinking blood?" he asked, with a frown upon his wrinkly old face.

"Yes, drinking blood. I'm pretty strong, too, and I'm fast. But drinking blood is kind of my main thing."

There was a pause and I could tell he was mulling it over. Obviously trying to think of how that could be used in a show. At that point in time, every carnival had a freak show. Some were better than others, but the best ones pulled in the crowds. People have always had morbid fascinations and before the world became a more politically correct place to live, no one was ashamed to tell their friends and neighbours about the oddities that they had witnessed. No one found anything wrong with it back in those days. I'm not saying that it was all good; it probably depended on the individual freak. Some had a better life after they joined the carnival and some had a worse life, but the same could be said for any of the human carnies, so it all seemed pretty fair.

"Vampiro! That's what we'll call you," came the outburst from the owner.

I knew at that very moment I hated the name. My real name is Eddie by the way. It used to be Edward, but I've been alive a long time and Eddie seems to fit in better with the modern day—when I'm not Vampiro, that is. I sat with the owner for a while—who, I later found out, was called The Great Waldo. I didn't mind my name quite as much when I found that out and as I got to know the other carnies, I realised most of them had stupid names. It was all part of the act and looked good on fliers that were distributed to promote the carnival. The Malcasa Carnival that I had joined was pretty standard, but what made them stand out from the rest was their freak show. They hired the best and they made sure that each of the freaks had their own show. Some were only a few minutes long and others went on for a while and had several carnies involved. Some were actually quite intricate and while I'd love to tell you more about some of those shows, those are stories for another day.

I slid right into carnival life and I loved it. Before I was a carnie—and since I had become one of the undead— I had been living in the shadows, moving from one place to another before the body count got noticed, but in the carnival, though we constantly moved, I was always home. There were other outcasts like me, those who were different. Hell, we were all different. Even the supposedly normal carnies didn't fit into everyday life. The owner or the Ringmaster, The Great Waldo, as I came to know him, had decided that my act would be to terrify the crowd. He had put me through some tests to make sure I really did drink blood, all with animals rather than people. That's how the show started. He would have me come on and bite the head off of a chicken and drink its blood. The main problem was that people weren't that freaked out. There were geeks in other carnivals that did the same thing. People had seen it before.

My second act was to drink blood from someone before the entire crowd. Now this one had me excited. All the time I had spent sneaking around in the shadows, only to be afforded the opportunity to have my meal in front of a large crowd. It was a bit of a dream come true and I was old enough that I could drink from humans without draining them completely. The problem with that act was, no one in the crowd wanted to volunteer so I would have to get one of the carnies to come on stage and let me drink some of their blood. People then believed it was all faked because it wasn't an audience member, so that act got canned pretty quickly, too. I can remember thinking at that point that I would probably never fit in anywhere. I had no memory of being turned into a vampire and had never met another of my kind, so I felt alone in the world. I had hoped that the carnies would become my family, but at that point I was concerned.

Act number three was a winner, though. I would prove I was a vampire by accomplishing feats that no human could. There were several ways of doing this, but the first one we tried that worked was to put me into a large chest with several poisonous snakes. The other carnies would then shake and kick the chest until the snakes went wild. When the lid was opened and I stood up they could see the snake bites all over my body. I could always hear the murmurs in the crowd.

"They aren't poisonous snakes."

He's already had the antidote before going in."

I bet he lies in a separate compartment from the snakes and those bite marks are fake."

I used to smile and watch their expressions change as the bite marks healed themselves in front of the crowd's eyes. Their murmurs would change to "oo's and ah's." It was a talking point for the crowd when they left the carnival and it helped spread word about us. The Great Waldo knew we had to add more to the act to keep it fresh.

I had an act where I was submerged in a glass tank of water and left in there while other acts went on. I would stay in the tank for over an hour sometimes. The punters would watch the other acts but I could see their eyes coming back to me. I didn't have to breathe so I could have stayed in there as long as I wanted, but it was pretty boring. I'd eventually come out just after one of the other acts finished to massive applause. The applause did nothing for me personally, but it did give me the reassurance that I would be staying with the carnival.

People come and go in a carnival. Sometimes people join and will travel with the carnival for years and others join and leave within a few months. I can remember one particular carnie named Melissa, who joined not long after me. She was quickly renamed 'Cobra, the Serpent Girl'. I was taken by her beauty the first time I saw her. She looked like any normal woman, but like me, she had fangs, though she wasn't a vampire. Snakes seemed to listen to her and as soon as she was near them, a calm would come over them all instantly. They did anything she told them to do and the crowd loved it. She was far superior to any snake charmer that they had ever seen and she quickly became a favourite act of the punters. I was mesmerised by her. She seemed both innocent and deadly. There was a quietness about her. However, wielding an army of snakes gave her a great deal of power in my eyes, not that she ever used it. It took me a while to pluck up the courage to approach her, but when I finally did, we hit it off. I didn't come onto her. We just became friends. Although we were treated well at the carnival and for all the differences we had among us, some of the other carnies were still scared of us both. We spent a lot of time walking between the tents and stalls just looking up at the night sky. She had a fascination with the gods and would spend hours telling me about various snake gods from different cultures. As time passed, I knew I was deeply in love with her, but the risk of pushing her away was too great so I never tried to make us anything more.

The acts Melissa and I performed did well for a while, and then the carnival started to struggle again. Carnivals tend to do that. Things are good for a while and then it tends to die off a bit. While both of our acts had been some of the most popular, as we continued to travel a similar route year after year, most people had seen them. Little did I know how much things were going to change and soon.

We had stopped at a few small towns and had pretty poor turnouts. Melissa and I were relaxing in my small caravan after a long walk when the Great Waldo appeared at my door. He let himself in as he always did though the caravan belonged to me. I bought it with my earnings, but I suppose Waldo believed he had a right to go wherever he wanted in his carnival.

"Vampiro," he said, then sighing before he carried on, as he always did when he had bad news. "Takings are down. Your act isn't pulling in as much money as it used to. I have a new idea and I want you to hear me out on it."

"Okay, let's hear it," I said, holding back my own sigh.

"We have this new guy, a clown. I haven't given him a name yet. The thing is, he seems a bit unhinged."

"What do you mean 'unhinged'? Aren't all clowns a bit crazy? Doesn't it come with the territory?" I asked.

"No, I mean yeah, but not like this guy. He's a monster. Looks like he has steroids with his cornflakes. Wears the regular clown makeup, but his costume's a little strange. Gives me the creeps, but we need new acts." The Great Waldo shivered as he finished speaking.

"What's all this got to do with me?"

"Well, I was thinking you could maybe fight him. I asked him what he does and he said whatever. Doesn't actually have an act. He's a big guy, though, and scary looking and you're super strong. I thought it would be a good crowd pleaser. Everyone loves a fight and a vampire going at it against a scary clown could be a winner."

"You want me to fight a fucking clown! Are you serious?"

"I'm telling you, it could be big. Think about it: Vampiro VS... uh... Koko... um, the Vampire- Killing Clown! It will sell out."

"I think you have lost it, and I thought you hadn't named him yet?"

"Yeah, well. I've named him now. He's a clown... and a vampire killer. People love cheese. They will lap it right up."

"What if he gets hurt? You know how strong I am."

"Oh, don't worry about that. Judging by the look of him, he's the kind of guy who gets off on pain."

"Great, I can't wait!" I said sarcastically.

"I'll set it up. This will get us back on top." And with that he left. Not a thank you or anything.

It was a few weeks before it was all set up. The Great Waldo had to get fliers drawn up and printed and then distributed all over the next town we were traveling to, to build up some hype. He was right, though. People do love a fight and they love a bit of cheese as well. The fight sold out as soon as we opened up. The Great Waldo had kept Koko under wraps. As unbelievable as I found it, I hadn't managed to get a single look at this supposedly psychotic-looking clown yet.

We were the main show, starting at eleven in the evening. A standard boxing ring had been set up in one of the larger tents and seats had been placed all around it. Most of the other carnies were there. They were being used as extra security to stop those without tickets from trying to sneak in and to be available just in case things got rowdy outside of the ring. The carnival wasn't in the habit of running boxing matches and the Great Waldo didn't know what to expect, so he had made sure he had plenty of support that night in the hope that everything would run smoothly.

I was first into the ring. I had brought Cobra, but no one else. I didn't think there was much point. It was a show and that was all. My biggest worry was that I ended up accidentally hurting Koko. I'd have to pull my punches but still make it look good or everyone would demand their money back.

When Koko came out and I saw him for the first time, I was shocked. He was at least seven feet tall and he *did* look mental. His torso was covered in a typical red, yellow and blue clown suit but he had ripped the arms from it, possibly because his arms would have been too large to fit. He had muscles on his muscles. I had never seen anyone of such proportions. He had clown make up on his face, white with red, and black diamond eyes. His hair was the colour of fire and styled into thin spikes. I could see what Waldo had meant about him looking like the kind of guy who might enjoy pain. He was definitely the most psychotic- looking clown I had ever seen. He jumped into the ring and just started pacing back and forth on his side. He looked like he wanted to murder someone. Me, probably, but I was hoping he was just a great actor rather than his taking this all too seriously.

The bell rang and he almost sprints across the ring at me. I put my guard up high and he smashes me in the ribs. Now, my organs are useless. I have no real need for them; they are just still there. The blood keeps me alive, but when that first punch landed, I felt like I was going to die, as if something inside was going to stop working. I knew right then that this was no human clown. He was something else. I pulled my guard lower as he threw body shots while I tried to recover. He then caught me with a right hook to the jaw that nearly took me off my feet. I started to move around the ring, keeping my distance, but he moved quickly for something so large. I'm not going to take you through the fight, blow by blow, but it went on pretty much like this throughout. He attacked and I was on the defensive... not how I had anticipated things would have gone. It was scheduled for fifteen rounds since that was standard for big fights back then. By the time we got to round ten I was on shaky legs. I had never experienced anything like this in all my time as a vampire, and I had never been put under such physical exertion or pain, either.

Round eleven started and I was wondering if I could do five more rounds. That was the round that Koko went absolutely berserk. He started grabbing me around the neck and throwing knees into my ribs. When the referee tried to intervene, Koko threw him from the ring into the crowd. Most of the crowd was on its feet. They had never seen a fight like this one. I threw a few elbows and one that caught the clown in the temple rocked him, giving me time to throw a series of body blows. It almost seemed like he was absorbing the pain. The last thing I remember is him grabbing me around the neck again and smashing his knee into my forehead—and it was lights out.

I came around about ten minutes later. The carnies were trying to clear the tent. There were screams and shouting. Cobra was kneeling over me smiling, but she had tears in her eyes. I later found out that when Koko had knocked me out, he had dropped on top of me and started raining blows down onto my face. Cobra had immediately leapt the ropes and fly- kicked him, her boot hitting him squarely in the chest. He had barely budged, as she tells it, but he did stop his assault on me to focus on her. She had tried to circle the ring, but he lunged at her and grabbed her by the throat. He lifted her off of the canvas, squeezing the life out of her with both hands... and then they were on him. Snakes. At first there were only a few, but they kept coming. The carnival had their own snakes, but they were coming from the surrounding fields, too. Koko had over one hundred snakes latched onto him in a matter of seconds, several different venoms pumping into him at the same time. Cobra was smiling down at him, even before his grip loosened. Seconds later he was lying dead on the floor with Cobra standing over him. The snakes quickly departed. It didn't take me long to recover. I drank from a few different people and I was good as new. It made me wonder, though. I had considered myself immortal and it was almost all over, just like that. I tried to form a relationship with Cobra after that, something more than just a friendship, but she rejected my advances and eventually left the carnival. I wanted to go with her, but she had snuck away in the night. I think she loved me too, but for one reason or another, she had decided that it was best we parted ways. I'll never forget her and I will always be grateful for the day she saved my life.

Things were never the same after her departure and soon after, the Great Waldo died. He had kept us going for as long as he could, but the outside world had already put him under pressure to change the way the carnival was run. Once he had passed away the new owners swooped in and got rid of half of the old carnies and replaced them with people who had no idea how a carnival should be run, kids who were cheap to hire. I think the only reason they kept me was because I was still young and fit. It's true that vampires don't age.

The world changed, too. Carnivals can't have freak shows anymore. They would have protesters crawling all over them and it would be a PR nightmare. On top of that, technology had taken over kids' lives and a trip to the carnival wasn't a big deal anymore. Young couples didn't go on dates to the carnival like they used to. I had ideas to revitalise the carnival, but the new owners didn't listen to me. It was a business for them, not a lifestyle like when the Great Waldo was in charge. I had been relegated to running one of the little amusement arcade tents. My acts were useless in the modern carnival. They barely had any shows anymore. The people that did come, came for the rides or to eat junk food and often just to wander around and barely spent a penny. There were still things we could have done to bring in more of a crowd, but what did I know? I was just an old act. For months I ran the amusement arcade wondering how I should approach the owners, how could I make them understand that the carnival could be grand once again, but in the end I knew it would never happen. I wasn't ready to let my dream go so easily. If the new owners didn't want to listen, they would need to go. I had thought about different ways of going about it, but each scenario resulted in my being found out and captured or killed. I took my time and I went about my day- to-day life as I pondered how I could bring real change... and then it struck me. I would create more of my kind and use the new vampires to replace everyone in the carnival. If we could take them all out in one evening and move on, leaving no one to talk of what happened, surely I couldn't be caught. I'd have enough people to run the carnival so I wouldn't need to bring in anyone new. It seemed foolproof. The main problem with it was that I didn't know how to make another vampire.

I decided the best way to work it out would be to start trying out methods I had seen in movies or read in books. I began working my way through them, but it took a while. I never wanted to kill more than one person per town and I'd often try and leave a few towns between kills. I can drink from people without killing them, so I only kill if I choose to, rather than out of necessity. The thirst lessens as each year passes. Since I didn't know what I was doing, I accidently killed quite a lot of people, but as I said, I had to spread it out, so it took me a few years to finally get it right. Once I had perfected the method, it was easy enough for me to start turning people, but I also couldn't just turn half a town, so I slowly began to collect my new family. One thing I hadn't planned for was how thirsty new vampires are. It was a nightmare keeping them fed without drawing any attention to myself. I kept them in my trailer at first. It was dark, for obvious reasons and there was space, but as my family grew, I had to start keeping them in the back of one of the empty trucks and I had to move them out before we moved town every time. It was a lot of work, but as each day passed, I felt happier and happier. I was going to take the carnie back to days gone by. The world never stops changing and moving. No matter how nostalgic everyone gets, we can never go back. It's a strange thing. Well... I'm going to set the clocks back. The new carnies will do things my way. We will have a freak show once again. When the entire carnival is run by vampires, no one will challenge us. No one will stand in our way. We will go from town to town and we will do things my way. My children will hunt and I will create more of my kind. Of course, it won't say any of that on the flier. Who would come? It will say something cheesy, like, 'Vampiro & the Carnival of Vampires.' The Great Waldo would have liked that.

The End

A Town Called Easter

By

Kevin J. Kennedy

Nikki opened the picnic basket up and started setting out the various jams, marmalades, breads, cheese and crackers while Richard opened up the bargain basement bottle of bubbly they had bought for the occasion. They had been together for three months, each having spent a considerable amount of time single, recovering from their own bad relationships. It had been Richard's idea to get away for the day. He had never been the most romantic of men, and was trying to make sure that Nikki knew how much he appreciated her, even though he wasn't the best at showing it all the time. Neither of them had much money, so this had seemed like a nice option.

"Did you bring any chocolate spread?" Nikki asked Richard.

"Uh, no. I thought we would act posh and have crackers n cheese and stuff like that," Richard said, grinning.

Nikki playfully punched him in the arm. "You're an idiot. Why'd you get all this stuff? You could have just gotten some crisps and some drinks and I'd have been happy," she told him, giving him her award-winning smile. She was different from all the girls he had been with before. Nicer, less fake. He had never met anyone before with whom he was so happy to spend so much time at home. They rarely left the house anymore, other than to go to work.

"I thought you deserved a treat," Richard responded.

"Oh, yeah, and what did I do to deserve this treat, might I ask?"

As she looked up at Richard from her seat on the tartan blanket they had laid down when they arrived, she could see he was no longer looking at her, but staring past her instead, into the distance. A quick glance over her shoulder showed her nothing.

"Hey! Am I boring you?" Nikki asked, half joking, half annoyed.

No answer came straight away, but Nikki could see the look on Richard's face change.

"Get up! Get up now!" Richard urged, leaning forward and grabbing her around the wrist, and yanking her from her seat.

"Hey! What the fuck?" Nikki snapped, tugging her wrist back, but Richard didn't let her go.

"We need to run, Nikki! Now!" and with that Richard turned and started to run, pulling her with him. As Nikki started running, having no real other option as Richard had no intention of letting her go, she managed to look back over her shoulder without falling and what she saw almost made her stop in her tracks. Although her mind filled with utter disbelief, she picked up her pace, and overtook Richard. Seeing that she was no longer fighting it, Richard let her wrist go, as she passed him, and picked up his own pace. The herd bearing down on them, was enough incentive for both to move at their top speed. Neither of them looked behind them as they sprinted towards the car that seemed to be their only protection.

Both Richard and Nikki crashed into the side of the car, not having slowed down enough on approach. Richard had already dug the keys out of his pocket but fumbled to get them in the lock.

"Fucking open it!" Nikki screamed, her voice high and whiny. "Quick! They're almost here!"

Richard grabbed her, and pushed her inside as he opened the door, diving in on top of her, and slamming it shut behind him. As the door slammed shut, there were three loud bangs, and the car shook with each. The animals smashing into the vehicle were roughly the same size and weight as wild boar, but looked completely different. They were covered in white fur, had pointy ears, and massive incisors. Other than the fact that they looked like they would tear most dogs apart, they looked pretty rabbit-like. Their legs were more like a dog's, but much more muscular, and their entire snouts were covered in scraggly- looking whiskers. There was the sound of metal bending as more of them smashed against the car, and the rattling of their massive nails, tapping the glass as some of them started to stand on their back legs, and look in through the side windows.

The engine roared to life, with Richard scarcely in his seat. It had been a struggle untangling himself from Nikki, the way they had jumped into the car, but he knew that time was of the essence. Jamming the gear stick into first gear, he stomped his foot on the accelerator, as he let the clutch up. The car began to wheel-spin in the still-damp grass, before catching and jerking forward. Just as the car stared to move, one of the giant rabbit-looking creatures came crashing through the back window. The glass erupted inwards, and covered both driver and passenger. Nikki screamed and Richard struggled to keep control of the car, as he headed back to the dirt track that brought them into the field.

"Nikki, do something. I can't let go of the wheel. There's a Maglite in your door." Nikki, having no idea what a Maglite was, and barely able to take her eyes off the monster that was halfway into the vehicle, nevertheless, quickly turned towards her door and looked in the tray. The only thing there was a massive metal torch. Nikki didn't give a fuck if it was the Maglite or not. She hurriedly wrapped her hand around the bottom of it, and turned back quickly. The beast was dragging itself further through the glass. Its white fur matted now, with red blood leaking out from where the broken window had cut it. Nikki quickly swung the torch as hard as she could, and connected with the front of its snout. She could feel the teeth crunch through the metal of the torch. The creature let out a horrific screech, before snapping at her. Several of its front teeth were now broken at awkward angles, but it just made it look all the more frightening. Nikki screamed as loud as she could but this time it wasn't high and shrill; it was filled with rage. She leaned further into the back of the car and started to repeatedly smash the torch down onto the thing's skull. The glass and bulb on the torch had broken with the first strike, but the solid metal was showing no sign of giving in. Her hand hurt, as she repeatedly struck the top of the creature's skull, but with each strike, it was receding back, out of the window. With one last mighty swing, she knocked the beast nearly unconscious, as it fell backwards through the glass. Unable to keep its footing, it slid off the boot and into the grass, knocking over a few of the others who were following.

With the extra traction beneath the tires as it hit the dirt track, the car picked up speed, leaving the animals howling and screeching behind them.

***

The two men stood, facing each other, in the middle of the military-style canteen. The compound was top of the range. Five of them had put up the cash to have it built, and moved in as soon as it was finished. The world was changing faster than ever and they were prepared for whatever came next. There were fifteen families, total, living there now. The compound had been built just a few miles from a little town called Easter, with a population of just over two thousand. They rarely went into the town, but it was handy having it nearby, just in case. Most of what they needed was delivered in bulk, directly to the compound.

"What the fuck do you mean, 'they can't die'?" Tom, one of the initial five, asked Simon.

"We've been shooting them from the compound roof. They go down, but they get back up, in less than a minute. There were seven of us. Didn't take us long to put them down, but before we knew it, they were back up and attacking the gates. One of them was completely missing the top of its skull, and it was still throwing itself at the gate," Simon replied.

"I need to see this for myself. Let's go." And with that, they left the room.

***

Sam sat slumped in his chair, his back aching from years of bad posture. The local newspaper office was quiet, as always. Only the funding from the town hall kept them operational. There wasn't all that much news in a town the size of Easter, but the mayor felt that every town should have a local paper, so it continued printing reports of who was pregnant, and who had died, even though everyone already knew before the paper hit the stands. He sipped at his frozen cold, strong black coffee as he stared out the glass front to the small office. The street outside was quiet as always, when the phone began to ring. *Wonder who's pregnant or dead this time?* Sam thought to himself. As the day progressed, the phone would continue to ring off the hook, long after Sam was dead.

***

"What the fuck do you mean, they just escaped?" Dr. Arrivel, asked Winston.

"They got out boss. I'm sorry. It was my fault. It's... you know... the Valium. My mind's so cloudy. It's my fault. I'm sorry," Winston cowered in the corner, as he admitted his umpteenth fuck-up to his boss. He knew the punishment would be severe; more so this time, than ever. He knew it had taken Dr. Arrivel years to perfect the Chaos Rabbits, and now they were gone, all of them.

"Do you know what you have done, Winston? Letting those things loose?" his boss said putting his head in his hands. Winston was surprised that his boss hadn't struck him immediately, followed by a sound beating.

"I'll get them back, boss. I promise. I just wanted to wait, and let you know what's happened.

"Get them back! Do you know how many of them there will be already? Do you know how quickly they breed? This town will be gone by the morning, and then the next, and the next. We have to get out of the country, and now!" and with that, Dr. Arrivel turned, and left the room quickly, leaving Winston standing alone, unsure of what to do. After a few seconds, he rushed out of the room, quickly following his boss.

***

"What the fuck *were* those things?" Nikki asked, in a panicked voice, as they sped down the dirt track. She kept looking behind them, but it didn't seem like the things were following.

Richard stared straight ahead, a look of determination on his face as he tried to keep the car on the track, driving a lot faster than anyone had in a long time on this narrow, half-road.

"I'm not sure they have a name, babe. They look pretty new. I think if they had been around for a while, Attenborough would have been all over that shit. Let's get back to town, and go straight to the police station."

"What, exactly, do you think old Bert is going to do about a hoard of killer rabbits, the size of dogs, Richard?" Nikki retorted, in a harsh tone.

"I don't fucking know, Nikki," Richard snapped back, then continued, "but *I* certainly don't fucking know what to do about them." It was the first time Richard had snapped at Nikki since they met and he regretted it, instantly, but the situation was far from normal and under the circumstances, he felt he shouldn't be too hard on himself. They were alive, and from the looks of things, they had escaped death. He would make it up to her as soon as they were out of this crazy situation.

***

"See, I told you." Simon, said to Tom, as the two men looked out at the compound gates. "They just keep attacking the fence. It may be reinforced, but eventually it's going to give. Doesn't really matter, now. Everyone is inside, and the place is on lockdown. They will never make it through the walls, even if they do get through the fence. The electricity running through the fence hasn't bothered them since we first shot them, but they seem to be learning. They have started to dig under the gate."

Tom took off his mirrored glasses, something Simon couldn't remember seeing before. The boss was one of those guys who wore his sunglasses in dark rooms. He looked towards Simon.

"I think this is the end of times, son."

Simon wasn't Tom's son. Tom called everyone 'son', even though he was only forty-eight himself.

"The end of times, boss?"

"There are giant fucking bunny rabbits attacking our electrified fence, some of which have parts of their skulls missing, with brains dripping out, and yet they still move. It's Easter fucking day and I've heard nothing of this on the news, which means this fucked-up situation started in a little town called Easter. Either somebody is about to make a fucking reappearance, or my name isn't Tom fucking McCallum."

***

Bazingo's friends all thought he was a bit mental. What was the point in being a clown in a town so small, with anywhere else so far away, that he would never make the journey? Bazingo, thought *they* were all mental, though. Clowns got a bad rap. Everyone thought they were creepy fuckers, scary; there were even people who had a phobia of them, what the fuck? Bazingo would make sure that, at least the kids of Easter town knew that clowns were people, just like everyone else. He spent more time online with his clown buddies these days, than he did in the outside world. His clown buddies understood him; he had even been invited to a few interesting clown circles that he never knew existed.

Backstage in the church hall, the only place in town that held any type of show outside of the town hall, he applied the finishing touches to his makeup. He always went with the predominately white face with a big red smile and rosy cheeks, no sad face or tears. He was a happy clown; he brought joy.

The church doors were never closed; the priest didn't believe in it. The church was for everyone, and he wanted people to know that. The rabbits' arrival went unnoticed by anyone. The church was still empty, other than Bazingo and the priest, but the priest had gone to search the rafters for some of the Easter props for the kids. Bazingo never heard the three oversized bunnies appear. Two still alive, saliva dripping from their massive incisors, the other was missing it's lower jaw, making it look even more terrifying than the others. It had no way to bite anymore but the massive bone-like claws, extending from its split paws were still deadly.

Bazingo, finishing applying the makeup, turned to see the three monsters standing in a semi-circle around him. The smile disappearing from his face barely showed through the makeup.

"What the fu……."

Bazingo's words were cut off by one of the live rabbits diving at him and burying it's teeth into his throat. The other two were on him before he hit the ground. The other live rabbit creature gnawing at his innards as the dead rabbit moved through the church sniffing out the preacher. When the two live rabbits were finished with Bazingo, the sight he left was not one that would put a smile on children's faces.

***

The first rabbit, the one they had been testing on from the beginning sat hunkered in the cave. They had never been able to move it. It had given birth many times, each time to more deformed kits and most had been killed by the two humans that kept them. The last two litters had been much larger, both in number and size of the kits. All had survived and been caged by the humans. When they had seen their chance to escape, watched only by the buffoon assistant they had taken it. She was much larger than the others. She had survived for centuries in a cave on the coast of Scotland, happy in her life alone, often only visited by the gulls and sea creatures. She needed to eat rarely but when she did she would often be brought food by the passing wildlife. She was the mother of all known species in the Leporidae family, the first of her kind, the mother of them all. She needed no mate to breed, but when they started experimenting on her, that's when things had changed. They had inseminated her with all manner of animals and the results had been monstrous but it mattered not to her. She didn't understand modern values or religions or morals. She knew only that the kits were her children, her family and she needed as many of them to survive as possible. They had somehow sped up her cycle so she was almost constantly pregnant and with each new litter, the kits seemed to grow smarter. They grew to full size so fast and then they left her but she would have more, many more. As she went into labour, she could tell instantly that the newest batch of kits would be the largest yet.

***

Richard punched his foot down on the brake, causing the car to screech along the tarmac and stop only inches from the front of the small police office. He turned the engine off and jumped out of the car, leaving the door hanging open. "Come on." He said, waving Nikki with him as he burst thought the door, into the police office to find old Sam, asleep in his chair.

"Sam!" Richard shouted, causing Sam to sit up quick and spill his coffee all over his desk.

"For fuck sake, Richard! You'll give a man a heart attack. What in hell's blazes has got you acting so crazy? You on drugs, boy?" asked the old cop, trying to look stern, while gathering his thoughts at the same time.

Just as Sam started to mop up the mess on his desk, the phone started ringing. He picked it up and Nikki and Richard watched as his face showed the confusion of what he was hearing.

"Giant rabbits, Mavis? Have you been drinking again?" he paused for a second and they could hear Mavis giving Sam the 'what-for' over the phone. "Okay Mavis, I'll be right over. Just you stay inside." And with that, he put the phone down. "Now, as you can see I'm pretty busy, so if you could just tell me why you came barging into my office like bats-out-of-hell, you can be on your way."

"We saw them, the rabbits. That's what we came here to tell you. There are loads of them and they are massive," said Nikki, rushing to get her words out. "They rammed our car."

"Rabbits rammed your car?" Sam asked, in a disbelieving voice. He pushed passed the young couple shaking his head, as he made his way to the door. "Maybe I'll catch myself some dinner on my rounds. Been a while since I had a nice rabbit stew." And he turned and pushed the door to the small office opened and was out on the street.

He had gone no more than two steps, when one of the creatures hit him, head height and took him to the ground. The beast landed on his chest and started ripping at his face, drowning out his screams as it tore the flesh from his face. Another joined it, quickly burying its claw in Sam's stomach and tearing his insides out. Soon, what little of Sam was left, couldn't be seen by Nikki and Richard, as there were at least fifteen of the monsters fighting for the scraps. It was quite a sight to behold. Some of the creatures had clearly been killed or badly wounded, but they moved amongst the others, their pace scarcely slowed. There was more variety among the herd, too. *Were they a herd or a pack?* Nikki wondered to herself. Some of the rabbit creatures were twice the size of the other German Shepherd-sized ones that they had seen earlier and while others were similar in size, they had less fur and it was darker. These were a lot more muscular than the rest, their tongues much longer, too. Some of their tongues must have been a foot in length.

Just as Richard was wondering whether their best option was to lock themselves in a cell and wait for help, the creatures' heads all turned away from the window at once, obviously distracted by something outside. Like some mutated plague of monsters, hopping over cars and crushing the metal beneath their feet as they went, in a second they were gone.

Nikki looked at Richard with tears in her eyes. "We're going to die, Richard, aren't we?"

"Not if I have anything to do with it," he said, grabbing her hand and pulling her to the door. He peeked outside and could see the street seemed empty.

"Okay, when we get outside, just run for the car and don't stop for anything.

***

Easter town centre wasn't all that large. A few shops, a hairdressers, a small bank and a bar. In the middle of the day, though, it was where most of the townsfolk were, for one reason or another. When the creatures descended, it was all-out carnage. Men, women and children were run down in the street and torn apart in seconds. The rabbit monsters were everywhere; the larger ones had taken to jumping through store windows to attack those inside and allow their smaller kin entrance.

Some of the townsfolk fought back, using whatever came to hand as weapons, but there were too many of the creatures-- there had to be hundreds. Those who fought, at best killed a few of the monsters, but they were quickly replaced by others and the rabbits that fell, got back to their feet only moments later. Some of the creatures were missing both eyes and yet they still went on, causing a path of destruction. Some of the creatures had most of the skin from around their mouths missing, causing the bone of their jaws to extend out; they looked absolutely horrifying. A few people made it to their cars and sped away, on route out of town or to pick up loved ones before leaving, but the rabbits gave chase, determined to leave no one alive.

***

Tom and Simon stood on the roof of the compound, surrounded by almost everyone else who lived there. Most had their rifle amongst several other fire arms. When the rabbits had made it through the gates, they had started picking them off, but it was more for fun than anything else. The men knew the creatures couldn't get inside the walls, and they were only down for a few moments, before getting back up; obviously, the bullets didn't stop them. They had killed a few of them using grenades, but as more and more of the things kept turning up, they decided to hold onto their ammo for the time being.

At first they had all agreed against calling outside for help. They didn't want any government officials snooping around the compound but, after a while everyone agreed that they needed the outside help They were entirely surrounded now by the things and the number seemed to keep growing. It seemed impossible, but the things seemed to give birth every few hours and the kits grew to full-size in an hour. It was unbelievable to watch. The call had been a hard one to make and the story was not pleasantly received, but they had done it. No one had come for them, though and there was no response from the other end, now. Could this be happening everywhere? Tom wondered, as he looked out into the distance to watch more of the creatures loping over the hill toward them.

***

Just outside the town limits, Richard pulled the car over to the side of the road, as the engine finally gave out.

"Oh my god! Richard, we can't stop here for fuck sake! We're in the middle of nowhere," Nikki said, with more than a little hint of fear in her voice.

"We've run out of petrol. I totally forgot. We were a bit distracted just trying to get out of there alive. I didn't have any more money for petrol. I spent the last of my cash on the picnic stuff." Although Nikki wanted to scold him, she also felt a little flutter in her heart. It lasted barely a second before the fear crept back.

"So what now?" Nikki asked.

"Well, I think we'd better start running. I don't know how much distance we put between them and us now, but it won't take them long to catch up. We need to find an old farm house or something because this car certainly wont keep them out."

"Fuck!" Nikki knew he was right. She just didn't want to believe it. Richard leaned over and pulled her in for a hug. With his arms round her he whispered in her ear. "Baby, I love you, but we need to go." And with that, they let each other go, got out of the useless vehicle and ran into the night.

***

As it got darker outside, everyone from the compound had vacated the roof and gone inside to either try and sleep, or get something to eat. Only Tom and Simon remained, looking out at what must have been thousands of the creatures loping around and attacking each other. The number of variations was hard to count, but Tom could swear there were at least thirty different species or types of the creatures, and that wasn't including the ones that he was sure had altered looks due to their injuries or deformities.

"You know. I think we will be okay in here, at least for a while." Tom said.

"What do you mean?" Simon asked

"Well. It's the end. No one survives the end but I think we have a while left."

"The end. Like of times? Like you said earlier?"

"Yeh"

"You believe in all that Bible crap?"

"Na, I don't believe any of the religions have it right. I do think someone started all this mad shit that we call life, but I think He is probably a bit bigger than the stupid shit we attach to Him. He's back and He's pissed. Whether man made these rabbits or not, it was in His plan. He's not '*a*' god, He's the only God. The One who started it all and the One who's decided to end it now. It always had to end with us. I thought He would let us fuck it all up for ourselves, if I'm honest. We didn't have long left anyway, considering the way the world is going but He's obviously bored with our shit. Or maybe it was something else. Who knows? I can barely stand any-fucking-one. God only knows how He tolerated billions of us.

***

Dr. Arrivel and Winston looked out to sea from the back of the ship. They had made their escape from the UK island, but they knew what they unleashed wouldn't stop there. They were only buying themselves time.

"You know Winston, I should have left you back there to die. You are the most useless excuse for a human being I have ever come across. I'm sure that those things will make it across the water somehow, but if they don't I'm going to need you to help me with something."

"Yes boss, yes boss, anything." Winston replied quickly, nodding as he did.

"I've heard rumours that an old hunter who lives in the Appalachian Mountains has real proof that Bigfoot exists. Maybe if we can get to him in time... Maybe... Yes. We can create an army. That's it. I'll be a hero, the saviour of the human race."

Winston didn't like the sound of it. His boss's ideas always involved kidnapping someone or something and things always turned out bad. Still, what else was he going to do? He had no home to go back to. The UK would be decimated. If he had just never told his boss about the giant rabbit in the cave, none of this would have ever happened.

***

As the rabbits savaged the last residents of the little town called Easter, a man sat in the cave alongside the giant rabbit. His side pressed into the rabbit's soft fur, gently stroking it, with a contented smile on his face. They looked out into the night sky and appreciated the stars more than either of them had ever appreciated mankind.

The End

Christmas in Hell

By

Kevin J Kennedy

You know, I always hated Christmas. It just wasn't for me. I hated that it had nothing to do with the religious side of it anymore and was basically a retail-run holiday in which everyone felt obligated to spend money they didn't have on shit that they gifted out to people who would never use it. Over the years I received some ridiculous gifts that I can only assume were recycled from the year before. Some of those gifts must have been in circulation for years now. If you didn't already know, lots of people stockpile the gifts they get that they consider to be shit, for want of a better word. These items remain in a closet for the next eleven months or so. Then the current owner decides to rewrap them in some new paper, add a new little name tag and hey—presto!—they spent fuck-all but still have a gift for your ass.

Everyone is a winner... well, except maybe you. You then need to hold onto that piece of shit until next year, until you can palm it off on some other unlucky asshole.

Anyway, I digress. 'Christmas is shit' was always my motto. I did enjoy time I spent with loved ones, but I always enjoyed that at any time of year. I enjoyed eating too much but then again, it's not like I'm exactly strict with my diet throughout the year. The time off of work was probably the only bit I really appreciated. I wasn't one of those Grinch-like assholes, though. I didn't spend the season telling others how it was all shit and try to get them to see things my way. People are entitled to do their own thing. Who am I to try and tell them what to enjoy and what to avoid? At the end of the day, I was roped into spending the same cash as everyone else and playing along, otherwise my wife and daughter would have killed me. Living with two women is never easy, but try disappointing them on a special occasion and just see how difficult your life becomes.

I suppose that brings us onto the point of my story. I'm in Hell. Not the 'my life is falling apart and I'm getting all dramatical about it' kind of hell…. like the actual, real Hell. It's not going to be one of those stories where I tell you that I'm not supposed to be here and then go on a mission to find my way out of Hell. Neither is it a story about me defeating some great evil, even though it means I need to stay in Hell forever. It's much less grand than that.

I arrived in October and it's now the twenty-fourth of December. Wherever Hell is, they celebrate Christmas here, too. *Of course they fucking do*, I can almost hear you saying. It's not for the same reasons people on Earth do, and what goes on is very different, but it's called Christmas none the less and it's celebrated on the same date. There is a Santa Claus of sorts and he does leave presents for some. Those are the main similarities. Everything else is a hellish parody of what I once knew and hated.

When I first arrived in Hell, I was sitting in a waiting room. The heating was turned up several times higher than any Earth-bound heating system could have achieved. I imagine the temperatures would have matched that of a furnace and yet there was no fire. The room was being heated by air vents pumping into the reception area. I wasn't sweating; I didn't catch on fire, but the discomfort I felt was insane. There was a desk with a sign above it saying 'Welcome to Hell'. I approached, but as I did the small creature behind the desk held up its paw and abruptly said, "We'll call you, please take a seat," before going back to its newspaper. I moved back to a seat and collapsed into it. My body was in no physical pain but the incredible heat was debilitating. After two hours of sitting around and getting more and more agitated, I approached the desk again. I got an identical response. When I tried to press the matter I was ignored. The small red creature that had been there before had gone and had been replaced by a slightly larger creature completely covered in blue fur. It reminded me of Cousin Itt from the *Addams Family* TV show. The creature was reading the same newspaper that the last creature had left behind. I went a little mental for a good few minutes, shouting at the new creature behind the desk but when it finally sunk in that the creature hadn't as much as raised its head, no security was coming for me and almost no one seemed to be paying any attention at all, I returned to my seat again.

After somewhere in the neighbourhood of twelve hours, my name was called. I rushed to the desk to be told to go into room six-six-six. Not only was it a cliché... it was the only room. I got into the room and sitting in front of me was one of the most gorgeous women I have ever seen. Apart from the two extra arms she was sporting, she was a perfect ten.

"Please take a seat," she told me.

I took a seat.

"Can you tell me why I'm here?" I asked her.

"You're here for your work assignment," came her reply.

"No, I mean why am I in Hell? Wait... what? My work assignment?" I asked, confused.

"Yes, your work assignment."

The conversation went nowhere fast.

I could take you over the hours and hours that we went around in circles but it would put you to sleep. What I can tell you is that I learned a few things. Firstly, no one in Hell is going to answer any of your questions. People will often give you pieces of information in general conversation, but never as an answer to a question that you asked. Secondly, time in Hell runs the same as it does on Earth, or at least it feels that way. What I didn't realise until a bit later is that when you aren't progressing with whatever is expected of you in Hell, time just stops completely and waits for you. It moves on when you do. The best example I can give you of this started occurring in noticeable scales when I began my first job.

My first job began directly after the meeting that I spent hours in trying to find out why I had a work assignment in the first place. When I left the little interview room, feeling pretty exasperated, I walked into a much larger room that held a mixture of people and creatures of various assortments that must have been in the thousands. Each sat in front of PC's with headsets on chattering away. A dippy-looking blonde girl with a too-large grin appeared next to me wearing a too-big t-shirt that read, 'welcome to the call centre'. *Typical,* I thought to myself. What else would be my given profession in Hell but a damn Telesales Advisor? I should have known. It turned out that for eight to twelve hours a day, I would be on the phones, cold calling people to try and sell them crap that they didn't need. The extra catch in Hell was that no one ever got a sale. Ever! I tried hanging up on customers that the system had called and put through to my line, hanging onto the call after the customer had hung up and various different techniques that were applied regularly in the call centre industry when you just couldn't be bothered. None of them worked. As I said earlier, if you weren't doing what you were supposed to be doing, time just stopped for you. It didn't seem to affect those around you, so I'm not quite sure of the logistics of it, but, still... time stopped all the same. Now everything was kind of irrelevant since it wasn't like anyone had anything better to do than to work at telesales all day, every day, with no chance of ever having a buying customer; 'tis tough on the mind. Oh, and we don't get weekends off. It's a seven- day- a- week number. We do get paid, though, and while it's Hell, there's no one here whipping and torturing us. As crazy as it sounds, some days I think I'd swap a day in the call centre for a savage whipping.

When I got off work from my first shift I was given a token for twenty hell notes. It was a fifth of my day's salary. Everyone was paid daily in Hell. You got a fifth of your salary and the rest went straight into your Christmas account. The money could only be lifted the week before Christmas and could only be spent on Christmas gifts. You couldn't even buy yourself one. We walked through a doorway that looked like it took you into another room, yet led, instead, into a park, I ranted loudly that this seemed like bullshit to me. I was informed that there was simply no way around it. The various call centre workers headed in every direction. I wasn't sure where any of the directions took you, so I just stood there looking dumb. After deciding it didn't really matter where I went, I just started walking in a straight line. I came to an edge of the park that was completely surrounded by a twenty-foot-high fence, dripping in barbed wire. There were three doorways with signs above them. They read, 'Halloween Land', 'The Gate' and 'Just Relax'. Obviously, I picked the one marked 'Just Relax' and quickly left the park.

To say it was a mistake would be an understatement. I spent the next fifteen or so hours being tortured before being released to go to work in the morning. I'm sure I died a few times, but each time something serious happened to my body it seemed like I blacked out and would wake up okay again... only for the torture to start all over. I was let go fifteen minutes before my shift began. I decided not to go into work and sat in the park for hours. After wandering around the perimeter of the park a few times and realising every door in the gate had disappeared, apart from the call centre one, I gave in and went to work. I thought maybe I would meet someone that could help me out a little. I was wrong. When I arrived, the shift was just beginning. Time had waited for me. I spent another day calling customers who wouldn't buy anything before leaving into the park again. I repeated this routine daily, every day finding new doors to try but each was as bad, if not worse, than the last. I thought a few times about just staying in the park, yet my mind kept niggling at me, whispering that one never knew if there might exist a good door to be found. When no one will answer any questions, it's difficult what to know about anything.

The weeks went by and I made no progress in discovering anything other than small quirks to Hell; nothing of any real use. They start celebrating Christmas in early November. That's one of the things that was hard to miss. I think it was around the tenth of November when I walked out the usual door at the end of my shift to find the park covered in fake snow with a massive Christmas tree in the middle. It was no different from Christmas trees on Earth in the way it was decorated. The only small difference was it leaked blood instead of sap. Although the actual day was a long way off and the money wasn't released for a while, it became apparent it was just another method of torture. Christmas songs played twenty- four hours a day or rather longer if time stopped for you for any reason. They played through the call centre headsets between calls, from speakers that were positioned everywhere, inside and out, and from the random places that the mystery doors took you to between shifts. Some of the songs I had liked in the beginning, others I'd always hated and some I'm sure had been made up badly on purpose just as an extra measure of pain. Not only did we have to listen to the shit non-stop, but we had to actually sing carols on breaks. The entire call centre had to stand at their desks and sing carols at the top of their lungs for both fifteen-minute breaks and their lunch as well. Not that any of them had to eat and no one went to the toilet in Hell, but it seemed to make the day even longer. I tried again to just not do it and my fifteen-minute break went on and on. I gave up in the end and sang along. Miraculously, in Hell, you will know the words to every single carol in existence, even if you didn't before.

As time passed, I realised that no one made friends in Hell; it was part of the plan. No one tried, although I'm sure everyone wanted to. I couldn't work out if the ones who seemed to have a little more control in the call centre were born in Hell or had been here longer. What granted them the privileged role of being able to wander about and occasionally talk to each other? But, really, who knows if they are actual conversations or just another strange goings-on of Hell? Our call scripts that we had to stick to, word-for-word on every call without deviation, suddenly changed. We were calling customers to sell them Christmas products at massively reduced prices. No one bought anything. I wondered if we were calling real people or if it was some kind of simulation that had us believing we were talking to someone. I seemed capable of independent thought. It was everything else that I had no control over. It was almost like I was watching a movie of myself having a shitty life but couldn't exert any control over the situation.

The weeks continued to pass and it finally it was the week before Christmas. The eighty percent of our salary that had been kept back was released to us in the form of a card with a Christmas parcel on the front. When I found the gates at the edge of the park on that night, each just said 'Presents' above it. I picked the middle gate for no reason other than I was standing in front of it. It took me to the largest department store I had ever seen. It was the stuff that nightmares are made from. Now, in case some of you think that sounds like a pretty fun evening, you're wrong. Shopping is an evil pursuit. You are surrounded with morons who pay no attention to where they are going, bump into you then look at you as if it's your fault. All the stores are always too hot, but, to be fair, pretty much everywhere is too hot in Hell. There are people looking for money from you for one thing or another on every corner. The queues are ridiculous, and stale alcohol reeks from those around you. I can't lie... I've never seen the attraction to being surrounded by a large crowd, and shopping often put me in a place where I hated everyone and everything. Now, that was my experience on Earth—in Hell it's so much worse. The shopping centre only plays the one Christmas song on repeat endlessly, so there is that to deal with. We all get a tour guide because the centre is so large. I got my ex-girlfriend. To say that she was an absolute bawbag on Earth would be an understatement, but, in Hell, she talks even more shit. None of what she says makes sense, not that it really ever did. She bursts into tears every twenty minutes or so and irrationally tells me how it's my fault—again, talking mainly gibberish that I'm not sure anyone would understand—and worst of all, I couldn't lose her. Every time I tried, I turned around and she was standing next to me.

Each day I'd try a different door in the park and every time I would be back in the same shopping centre with the same ex doing the same shit. This lasted until the day before Christmas, today. The day at work was the same as always. There was no party or games or anything else... just another shift of meaningless labour. As I walked out into the park, I thought something festive might be going on, but other than the tree and lights, it was the same. Everyone made their way to various gates on different sides of the park. I sat around for a while, wondering if I would have to spend the day with my ex again. I reasoned that surely Christmas Eve wouldn't be more shopping. When I got to the doors they read 'Griswold', 'Kingston Falls', and 'Hill Valley'. I had no idea what any of them meant, so I went into 'Hill Valley', thinking that it at least sounded like a nice place. It didn't so much take me anywhere as much as transport me into the future.

I found myself, on Christmas day, at a dinner with the Devil. The real one: big guy, red all over, horns, disproportionately large upper body with small legs. Yep, that's right, dinner with the Devil. Just him and me. I did wonder if somehow everyone had dinner with the Devil on Christmas day. Time there was strange and I'm sure he could have arranged it had he wanted to. I didn't imagine I was special. What I did find a little disconcerting was the Santa Claus costume he wore. It wasn't evil and terrifying, just the normal costume that Santa wore on Earth and it looked high- end. I can't imagine the Devil has money problems.

I just sat there looking at him. I wasn't sure what to say. We sat at either end of a long table. No one else was in the lavishly decorated room. After staring at him for a minute, wondering if I should say something, I realised this was the first time since I came to Hell that I wasn't being roasted. The room temperature was actually comfortable. It would appear that the Devil doesn't like it toasty.

Moments later a large set of doors opened and in came a troop of what looked to be female elves, apart from the fact that they were bright red like the Devil. Each was naked, wearing only sets of multi coloured Christmas lights. They carried trays of food which they placed along the table before disappearing back through the door. The Devil noticed me looking over everything.

"You can eat today, son."

My eyes quickly moved to him. "I thought no one ate in Hell."

"Well, you can eat today."

It wasn't exactly the in-depth sort of answer I was looking for but I was getting used to knowing next to nothing in this new life. I grabbed what looked to be a turkey leg and devoured it in a few bites, the juice dripping from my chin.

"Help yourself, boy, for tomorrow you go back to the start."

"What do you mean I go back to the start?" I asked.

"Back to the day you came here. You start all over again," he answered. He didn't eat. He just sat smiling and watching me.

"What the fuck? I need to go through all this shit again? What's even the point to it?" I bellowed, standing up and slamming my fists on the table. Fuck the Devil, right?

I did kind of regret it as soon as I had done it. I was waiting for him to spring across the table and rip my throat out, but he didn't—he didn't even move. He just waited for me to take my seat again. It was all a bit embarrassing if I'm being honest.

"Feel better?" he asked with a knowing smirk.

"A little," I answered honestly. It's always good to blow off a bit of steam, even if you do feel like a fool afterwards.

"Good. Now. I have a proposal for you."

"A proposal? Don't you control everything here?" I blinked in genuine surprise.

"No one controls everything anywhere, son. I'm looking for a replacement demon. One of my seasonal demons was killed and I need to get a replacement for next year. I gave my son a shot at it this year after he wouldn't stop hounding me about it, but he will make a mess of it like he does everything else. The lad is truly evil, but if I said he had shit for brains, I'd be insulting the shit. Anyway... the job. I need a new Krampus. You know who that is, right?"

I did, at this point, wonder if I was having the longest, weirdest dream of my entire life, but it was all too real. The smells and the details weren't dreamlike at all.

"You want me to be Krampus? The anti-Santa. Big blue guy that looks a bit like you and hates Christmas? Are you serious? Why the fuck would I want to do that?"

The whole set up in Hell is weird as shit, but this was next- level crazy.

"I've watched you. You've kept more of your own mind and memories than any of the others. I'm tired of replacing my minions constantly. You know, the saying that you can't get good staff is so true. I'm surrounded by idiots everywhere I go."

I had to remind myself that the Devil wasn't having a heart-to-heart with me. I wondered if he'd had one too many drinks before dinner.

"Why would I want to be one of your minions? No offence, but we aren't exactly well acquainted. Your back story precedes you and by all accounts, they say that you're a bit of an asshole. On top of all that, this place is insane. You're in charge. What about that says 'good boss' material?"

The Devil actually threw his head back and burst into a fit of laughter.

"Son, the way I see it, you can keep going back to the day you arrived and live through our extended Christmas season for eternity or, you can go through the transformation and return to Earth where you will hunt and kill throughout the Christmas season, year after year. Now tell me, which of those two ideas sounds like the most fun?"

I've got to be honest. The moral side of me was screaming at me to tell him where he could shove his job, that I could never take it, but if I'm truly honest with you, I just really hate Christmas.

As I said at the start, there is no great epiphany. I'm not going to spend eternity trying to redeem myself. In actual fact, I'm not all that sure what I did wrong to end up here in the first place. Either way, here I am, back on Earth, leaving my story for someone to find. It may become a new legend that parents tell their children and then pass into myth as time goes on or, maybe no one will ever read it. Who knows? I will tell you one thing, though. The next time I hear a Christmas carol, I'm going to tear everyone in the room to pieces. Merry Krampus.

The End

Afterword

Thank you very much for giving my second collection of short stories a go. I hope you enjoyed them. I've been at the writing game for a few years now and things are getting more series. I am fully aware I'm only able to do this thanks to people like you who pick up my book and give it a read, so, once again, thank you. If you have the time, please leave a little review on Amazon or Goodreads or even give the book a share on social media. It all helps and let's others know about my work.

Until the next book.

Kevin J. Kennedy